# CROSS CHANNEL

○

Presented by the

## Priscilla John
## Trust

PACIFIC
GROVE
PUBLIC
LIBRARY

# CROSS CHANNEL

## Julian Barnes

*Alfred A. Knopf* New York 1996

S

THIS IS A BORZOI BOOK
PUBLISHED BY ALFRED A. KNOPF, INC.

Copyright © 1996 by Julian Barnes

"Interference," "Experiment," and "Evermore" were
originally published in *The New Yorker*. "Gnossienne" and
"Dragons" were originally published in *Granta*.

Library of Congress Cataloging-in-Publication Data
Barnes, Julian.
Cross channel / Julian Barnes. — 1st American ed.
p.   cm.
ISBN 0-679-44691-5
I. British—Travel—France—History—Fiction.  I. Title.
PR6052.A6657C76  1996                              95-44427
823'.914—dc20                                          CIP

Manufactured in the United States of America
FIRST AMERICAN EDITION

TO  PAT

# INTERFERENCE

H E LONGED FOR DEATH, and he longed for his gramophone records to arrive. The rest of life's business was complete. His work was done; in years to come it would either be forgotten or praised, depending upon whether mankind became more, or less, stupid. His business with Adeline was done, too: most of what she offered him now was foolishness and sentimentality. Women, he had concluded, were at base conventional: even the free-spirited were eventually brought down. Hence that repellent scene the other week. As if one could want to be manacled at this stage, when all that was left was a final, lonely soaring.

He looked around his room. The EMG stood in the corner, a monstrous varnished lily. The wireless had been placed on the washstand, from which the jug and bowl had been removed: he no longer rose to rinse his wasted body. A low basketwork chair, in which Adeline would sit for far too long, imagining that if she enthused enough about the pettinesses of life he might discover a belated appetite for them. A wicker table, on which sat his spectacles, his medicines, Nietzsche, and the latest Edgar Wallace. A writer with the profligacy of some minor Italian composer. 'The lunchtime Wallace has arrived,' Adeline would announce, tirelessly repeating the joke he had told her in the first place. The

3

Customs House at Calais appeared to have no difficulty allowing the lunch-time Wallace through. But not his 'Four English Seasons'. They wanted proof that the records were not being imported for commercial purposes. Absurd! He would have sent Adeline to Calais had she not been needed here.

His window opened to the north. He thought of the village nowadays solely in terms of nuisance. The butcher lady with her motor. The farms that pumped their feed every hour of the day. The baker with *his* motor. The American house with its infernal new bathroom. He briefly thought his way beyond the village, across the Marne, up to Compiègne, Amiens, Calais, London. He had not returned for three decades – perhaps it was almost four – and his bones would not do so on his behalf. He had given instructions. Adeline would obey.

He wondered what Boult was like. 'Your young champion', as Adeline always characterised him. Forgetting the intentional irony when he had first bestowed this soubriquet on the conductor. You must expect nothing from those who denigrate you, and less from those who support you. This had always been his motto. He had sent Boult his instructions, too. Whether the fellow would understand the first principles of Kinetic Impressionism remained to be seen. Those damn gentlemen of the Customs House were perhaps listening to the results even now. He had written to Calais explaining the situation. He had telegraphed the recording company asking if a new set could not be dispatched contraband. He had telegraphed Boult, asking him to use his influence so that he might hear his suite before he died. Adeline had not liked his wording of that message; but then Adeline did not like much nowadays.

She had become a vexing woman. When they had first

been companions, in Berlin, then in Montparnasse, she had believed in his work, and believed in his principles of life. Later she had become possessive, jealous, critical. As if the abandoning of her own career had made her more expert in his. She had developed a little repertoire of nods and pouts which countermanded her actual words. When he had described the plan and purpose of the 'Four English Seasons' to her, she had responded, as she all too regularly did, 'I am sure, Leonard, it will be very fine', but her neck was tight as she said it, and she peered at her darning with unnecessary force. Why not say what you think, woman? She was becoming secretive and devious. For instance, he pretty much suspected that she had taken to her knees these last years. *Punaise de sacristie*, he had challenged. She hadn't liked that. She had liked it less when he had guessed another of her little games. 'I will see no priest,' he had told her. 'Or, rather, if I so much as smell one I shall attack him with the fire-tongs.' She hadn't liked that, oh no. 'We are both old people now, Leonard,' she had mumbled.

'Agreed. And if I fail to attack him with the fire-tongs, consider me senile.'

He banged on the boards and the maid, whatever was her name, came up at a trot. 'Numéro six,' he said. She knew not to reply, but nodded, wound the EMG, put on the first movement of the Viola Sonata, and watched the needle's stationary progress until it was time, with fleet and practised wrists, to flip the record over. She was good, this one: just a brief halt at a level crossing, then the music resumed. He was pleased. Tertis knew his business. Yes, he thought, as she lifted the needle, they cannot gainsay that. 'Merci,' he murmured, dismissing the girl.

When Adeline returned, she looked questioningly at Marie-Thérèse, as she always did.

'Numéro six,' replied the maid.

The first movement of the Viola Sonata. He must have been angry; either that or suddenly fearful over his reputation. She had come to understand the shorthand of his requests, to read his mood from the music he demanded. Three months ago he had heard his last Grieg, two months ago his last Chopin. Since then, not even his friends Busoni and Sibelius; just the music of Leonard Verity. The Second Piano Quartet, the Berlin Suite, the Oboe Fantasy (with the revered Goossens), the Pagan Symphony, the Nine French Songs, the Viola Sonata . . . She knew the articulations of his work as once she had known the articulations of his body. And she admitted that in general he recognised what was finest in his output.

But not the 'Four English Seasons'. She had thought, from the moment he had first talked about it, then blocked it out with his thinned fingers on the piano, that the scheme was misconceived. When he told her it was in four movements, one for each season, beginning with spring and ending with winter, she judged it banal. When he explained that it was not, of course, a mere programmatic representation of the seasons but a kinetic evocation of the memory of those seasons filtered through the known reality of other, non-English seasons, she judged it theoretical. When he chuckled at the notion that each movement would fit perfectly on the two sides of a gramophone record, she judged it calculating. Suspicious of the early sketches, she had liked the work no more in published form; she doubted that hearing it would convert her.

They had always agreed, from the beginning, to value

truth above mere social form. But when truths collide, and one of them is dismissed as the squalid personal opinion of an ignorant, foolish Frenchwoman, then perhaps there was something to be said for social form. Heaven knew, she had always admired his music. She had given up her career, her life, for him; but instead of weighing with him this now seemed to count against her. The truth was, she thought — and this was *her* truth — that some composers had a fine late flowering and others did not. Perhaps the elegy for solo 'cello would be remembered, though Leonard grew suspicious nowadays at her too frequent praise of it; but not the 'Four English Seasons'. Leave such things to Elgar, she had said. What she had meant was: you seem to me to be courting the country you deliberately left, indulging a nostalgia of the kind you have always despised; worse, you seem to be inventing a nostalgia you do not truly feel in order to indulge it. Having scorned reputation, you now appear to be seeking it. If only you had said to me, triumphantly, that your work would *not* fit on to gramophone records.

There were other truths, or squalid personal opinions, that she could not transmit to him. That she herself was not well, and the doctor had talked of surgery. She had replied that she would wait until the current crisis was over. By which she meant, until Leonard is dead, when it will not matter to me whether I submit to surgical intervention or not. His death had priority over hers. She did not resent this.

She did, however, resent being called a *punaise de sacristie*. She had not been going to Mass, and the idea of confession, after all these decades, struck her as grotesque. But everyone must approach eternity in their own way, and when she sat alone in an empty church she was contemplating extinction, not its palliation by ritual. Leonard would pretend not to see the difference. 'Thin end of the wedge,' he would say – had said. For her, it was simply that they adopted different stances before the inevitable. Of course he did not like or understand this. He was growing more tyrannical as he reached the end. The weaker his strength, the more he asserted it.

The fire-tongs sounded the opening of Beethoven's Fifth on the ceiling above. He must have heard, or guessed, her return. She ran heavily upstairs, banging an elbow on the turn of the banister. He sat in bed with the tongs aloft. 'Brought that priest of yours?' he enquired. But for once he was smiling. She fussed with his blankets and he pretended to object; but as she bent beside him, he laid his hand on her nape, just below her coiled and greying bun, and called her *ma Berlinoise*.

She had not anticipated, when they moved to Saint-Maure-de-Vercelles, that they would live quite so separately from the village. Pedantically, he had explained once more. He was an artist, did she not see? He was not an exile, since that implied a country to which he could, or would, return. Nor was he an immigrant, since that implied a desire to be accepted, to submit yourself to the land of adoption. But you did not leave one country, with its social forms and rules and pettinesses, in order to burden yourself with the parallel forms and rules and pettinesses of another country. No, he was an artist. He therefore lived alone with his art, in silence and in freedom. He had not left England, thank you very much, in order to attend a *vin d'honneur* at the *mairie*, or to tap his thigh at the local *kermesse* and offer a cretinous grin of approval to a squawking bugler.

Adeline learned that she must deal with the village in a swift and necessary fashion. She also found a way to translate Leonard's *profession de foi* into less rebarbative terms. M'sieur was a famous artist, a composer whose work had been played from Helsinki to Barcelona; his concentration must not be disturbed, lest the wonderful melodies forming within him be interrupted and lost for ever. M'sieur is like that, his head is in the clouds, it is just that he does not see you, otherwise, of course, he would tip his hat, why, sometimes he does not even notice me when I am standing in front of his face . . .

After they had been living in Saint-Maure for ten or so years, the baker, who played third cornet in the band of the *sapeurs-pompiers*, shyly asked her if M'sieur would as a special honour write a dance, preferably a polka, for their twenty-fifth anniversary. Adeline pronounced it unlikely, but agreed to put the request to Leonard. She chose a time when he was not working on a composition, and seemed to be of sunny temperament. Later, she regretted that she had not chosen a moment of foul temper. For, yes, he said, with a curious smile, he would be delighted to write a polka for the band; he, whose work was performed from Helsinki to Barcelona, was not so proud that he would not do such a thing. Two days later, he gave her a sealed manila envelope. The baker was delighted and asked her to convey his particular thanks and respects to M'sieur. A week later, when she entered the *boulangerie*, he would not look at her or speak to her. Finally, he asked why M'sieur had chosen to laugh in their faces. He had scored the piece for three hundred players when they had only twelve. He had called it a polka but it did not have the rhythm of a polka; rather, that of a funeral march. Nor could Pierre-Marc or Jean-Simon, both of whom had made some musical studies, discern the slightest melody in the piece. The baker was regretful, yet also angry and humiliated. Perhaps, Adeline suggested, she had taken the wrong composition by mistake. She was handed the manila envelope and asked what the English word 'poxy' meant. She said she was not sure. She pulled out the score. It was headed 'Poxy Polka for Poxy Pompiers'. She said she thought the word meant 'bright', 'vivid', 'shining like the brass on your uniforms'. Well then, Madame, it was a pity that the piece did not appear bright and vivid to those who would not now play it.

More years passed, the baker handed over to his son, and it was the turn of the English artist, the irregular M'sieur who did not even tip his hat to the curé when he met him, to ask a favour. Saint-Maure-de-Vercelles was just within range of the British Broadcasting Corporation. The English artist had a high-powered wireless that enabled him to pick up music from London. Reception, alas, was of greatly varying quality. Sometimes the atmosphere caused problems, there were storms and bad weather, against which nothing could be done. The hills beyond the Marne were not of great assistance, either. However, M'sieur had discovered, by deduction, one day when every single house in the village had fallen silent for a wedding, that there were also local forms of disturbance, from electric motors of all kinds. The butcher had such a machine, two of the farmers pumped their feed by this method, and of course the baker with his bread . . . Could they be prevailed upon, just for an afternoon, as an experiment, of course . . . Whereupon the English artist heard the opening bars of Sibelius's Fourth Symphony, that grave grumble from the lower strings and bassoons, which was normally below the threshold of audibility, with a sudden and refreshed clarity. And so the experiment was to be repeated from time to time, by permission. Adeline was the go-between on such occasions, a little apologetic, but also playing on the snobbery of the notion that Saint-Maure-de-Vercelles had living in its midst a great artist, one whose greatness embellished the village, and whose glory would shine the brighter if only the farmers would pump their feed by hand, the *boulanger* would confect his bread without electricity, and the butcher lady would turn off her motor as well. One afternoon Leonard discovered a new source of disturbance, which took powers of detection to locate and then delicacy of negotiation to disarm. The American ladies who were fair-weather occupants of that converted mill-house beyond the *lavoir* had naturally installed all manner of appliances, which in Leonard's view were quite superfluous to life. One of these in particular affected the reception on M'sieur's high-powered wireless. The English artist did not even have a telephone; but the two American ladies had had the decadence, and the impertinence, to install a water closet operated by electricity! It took a certain tact, a quality Adeline had developed increasingly over the years, to persuade them, on certain occasions, to delay their flushing.

It was difficult to explain to Leonard that he could not require the village to fold its shutters every time he wanted to listen to a concert. Besides, there were occasions when the American ladies simply forgot, or appeared to forget, the Englishman's demand; while if Adeline entered the *boulangerie* and found that the baker's old father, still third cornettist for the *sapeurs-pompiers*, was in charge, she knew there was little point in even asking. Leonard tended to become irate when she failed, and his normal pallor was blasted with puce. It would have been easier had he felt able to offer a word of direct thanks himself, perhaps even a small present; but no, he acted as if countrywide silence was his prerogative. When he first became seriously ill, and the wireless was transported to his bedroom, he wished to hear more and more concerts, which strained the sympathy of the village. Happily, over the last few months he had wanted nothing but his own music. Adeline might still be dispatched to obtain a vow of muteness from the village, but she would only pretend to go, confident that by the time the concert was due to begin Leonard would have decided not to bother with the wireless that evening. Instead, he would prefer her to wind up the EMG, shuffle the horn, and play him the Oboe Fantasy, the French Songs, or the slow movement of the Pagan Symphony.

Those had been brave days, in Berlin, Leipzig, Helsinki, Paris. England was death to the true artist. To be a success there you had to be a second Mendelssohn: that was what they were waiting for, like a second Messiah. In England they had fog between the ears. They imagined themselves talking about art but they were only talking about taste. They had no concept of freedom, of the artist's needs. It was all Jesus and marriage in London Town. Sir Edward Elgar, knight, Order of Merit, Master of the King's Musick, baronet, husband. 'Falstaff' was a worthy piece, there was fine stuff in the Introduction and Allegro, but he had wasted his time with Jesus, with those infernal oratorios. Parry! Had he lived long enough, he would have set to music the entire Bible.

It was not permitted to be an artist in England. You might be a painter, or a composer, or a scribbler of some kind, but those foggy brains did not understand the essential precondition behind all these subsequent professions: that of *being an artist*. In Continental Europe they did not laugh at such an idea. He had had fine times, brave days. With Busoni, with Sibelius. His walking tour in the Tyrol, when he had read his beloved Nietzsche in the German. Christianity preaches death. Sin is the invention of the Jews. Chastity produces as much foulness of soul as lust. Man is the cruellest animal. To pity is to be weak.

In England, the soul lived on its knees, shuffling toward the non-existent God like some butcher boy. Religion had poisoned art. 'Gerontius' was nauseating. Palestrina was mathematics. Plainsong was ditchwater. You had to leave England to find the upper slopes, to let the soul soar. That comfortable island dragged you down into softness and pettiness, into Jesus and marriage. Music is an emanation, an exaltation of the spirit, and how can music flow when the spirit is pegged and tethered? He had explained all this to Adeline when first he had met her. She had understood. Had she been an Englishwoman, she would have expected him to play the organ on Sunday and help her bottle jam. But Adeline had been an artist herself at the time. The voice had been coarse but still expressive. And she had seen that if he was to pursue his destiny, her art would have to be subordinate to his. You could not soar if manacled. She had understood that, too, at the time.

It was insistently important to him that she admire the 'Four English Seasons'. She was becoming ever more conventional and foggy between the ears: such was the penalty of age. She had at last spotted before her the great immensity of the void and did not know how to respond. He knew. Either you lashed yourself to the mast or you were carried away. He therefore kept ever more sternly and deliberately to the rigorous principles of life and art which he had spent so long enunciating. If you weakened, you were lost, and the house would soon enough contain the priest, the telephone, and the collected works of Palestrina.

When the telegram from Boult arrived, he ordered Marie-Thérèse not to mention the fact to Madame, on pain of dismissal. Then he placed an additional pencil cross against Tuesday's concert in the *Radio Times*. 'We shall listen to this,' he informed Adeline. 'Alert the village.' As she looked over his fingers at the paper, he could sense her puzzlement. A

Glinka overture, followed by Schumann and Tchaikovsky: hardly the preferred listening of Leonard Verity. Not even Grieg, still less Busoni or Sibelius. 'We shall discover what my young champion does with this old stuff,' he said by way of explanation. 'Alert the village, do you see?' 'Yes, Leonard,' she replied.

He knew it was one of his masterpieces; he knew that were she to hear it truly, she would recognise this. But it must come upon her suddenly. That opening enchantment of the remembered bucolic, with a pianissimo *cor anglais* wrapped in the quietest rustle of muted violas. He imagined the soft transformation of her face, her eyes turning towards him as they had done in Berlin and Montparnasse . . . He loved her enough to see it as his task to rescue her from her own later self. But there must be truth between them, too. As she straightened his blanket he therefore said, abruptly, 'This business won't be cured by *le coup du chapeau*, you know.'

She scurried from the room in tears. He could not judge whether they were caused by his acknowledgment of death or by his reference to their first few weeks together. Perhaps both. In Berlin, where they had met, he had failed to arrive for their second rendezvous, but instead of taking offence, as other women might have done, Adeline had come to his room and found him prostrate with an influenza cold. He remembered her straw hat, worn despite the lateness of the season, her full, clear eyes, the cool chord of her fingers, and the curve of her hip as she turned away.

'We shall cure you with *le coup du chapeau*,' she had announced. It was apparently some medical practice, or, more likely, superstition among the peasants of her region. She declined to elucidate, but went away and returned with a wrapped bottle. She told him to make himself comfortable and to put his feet together. When they formed a soft *puy* in the bed, she found his hat and placed it over his feet. Then she poured him a large tumblerful of cognac and told him to drink. At the time, he had preferred beer to strong liquor, but he did as he was told, marvelling at how improbable such a scene would be in England.

After two deep glasses, she asked if he could still see his hat. He replied that of course he could. 'Keep watching it,' she had said, and poured him a third glass. He was forbidden to speak, and had no memory now of what she had chattered on about. He merely drank and watched his hat. Finally, midway through his fifth glass, he had started to giggle and announced, 'I can see two hats.'

'Good,' she said with sudden briskness. 'Then the cure is working.' She had played the same spread chord on his forehead and left, taking the bottle with her. He fell into a coma and awoke twenty hours later, feeling much better. Not the least reason for this was that when he opened his eyes and looked down towards his feet there was no hat to be seen but only the profile of his already beloved Adeline, sitting in a low chair reading a book. It was then that he told her he was going to become a great composer. Opus 1, scored for string quartet, flute, mezzo-soprano, and sousaphone, would be called 'Le Coup du Chapeau'. Using his newly discovered method of Kinetic Impressionism, it would depict the travails of a suffering artist cured of influenza and lovesickness by a beautiful helpmeet and a bottle of cognac. Would she accept the dedication, he had asked. Only if she admired the piece, she had replied with a flirtatious tilt of her face.

'If I write it, you will admire it.' The statement was not vain or authoritarian but, rather, the reverse. Our destinies, he meant, are now joined, and I shall consider worthless any composition of mine that fails to please you. This is what his words intended, and she had understood.

Now, downstairs in the kitchen, stripping the fat from some beef bones to make Leonard's bouillon, she remembered those first few months in Berlin. How jolly he had been, with his cane, his sly wink, and his repertoire of music-hall songs; how not at all the stiff Englishman of racial stereotype. And what a different patient he had made in those days when she had given him *le coup du chapeau*. That had been the start of their love; now she was tending him once more, at the end of it. In Berlin, when he was recovered, he had promised that she would be a great singer and he would be a great composer; he would write his music for her voice and together they would conquer Europe.

It had not happened. She had doubted her own talent more than she doubted his. They made instead an artists' pact. They bound themselves together, twin spirits in life and in music, though never in marriage. They would fly free of the constraints that governed most people's existences, preferring the higher constraints of art. They would rest lightly on the ground so that they might soar the higher. They would not entangle themselves in the pettinesses of life. There would be no children.

And so they had lived: in Berlin, Leipzig, Helsinki, Paris, and now in a softly scooped valley north of Coulommiers. They had rested lightly on the ground here for over two decades. Leonard's fame had grown, and with it his reclusiveness. There was no telephone in the house; newspapers were forbidden; the high-powered wireless was used only for listening to concerts. Journalists and acolytes were denied entry; most letters went unanswered. Once a year, until Leonard became ill, they would travel south, to Menton, Antibes,

Toulon, incongruous locations where Leonard would fret for his damp valley and the lonely rigour of his normal life. On these journeys Adeline would sometimes fall prey to a sharper lamentation, for the family she had quarrelled with all those years ago. In a café her glance might pause on the face of some lyrical young man, and she would briefly consider him an unknown nephew. Leonard dismissed these speculations as sentimental.

For Adeline the artistic life had begun in gregariousness and warmth; now it was ending in solitude and austerity. When she had nervously suggested to Leonard that they might secretly be married she had implied two things only. First, that she would be better able to protect his music and watch over his copyrights; and, second, selfishly, that she would be able to live on in the house they had shared for so long.

She explained to Leonard the inflexibility of the French law in respect of concubinage, but he did not want to hear. He had become irate, banging the fire-tongs on the boards, so that Marie-Thérèse came running. How could she think of betraying the very principles of their life together? His music belonged to nobody and to the whole planet. Either it would be played after his death or it would not, depending upon the intelligence or stupidity of the world; that was all there was to be said. As for herself, he had not realised when they had made their pact that she had sought pecuniary advantage, and if that was what exercised her, she should take what money she could find in the house when he lay on his deathbed. She might as well return to her family and pamper those imaginary nephews she was always bleating about. Here, take the Gauguin off the wall and sell it now if that is your concern. But do stop your wailing.

'It is time,' Leonard Verity said.

'Yes.'

'We shall see what my "young champion" is made of.'

'Oh, Leonard, let us have the Oboe Fantasy again.'

'Just turn it on, woman. We are nearly at the hour.'

As the wireless slowly warmed and hummed, and the rain played a soft pizzicato on the window, she told herself it did not matter that she had failed to alert the village. She doubted he would persist beyond the overture to 'Ruslan and Ludmilla', which in any case had sufficient stridency to pierce most atmospheric disturbance.

'Queen's Hall . . . Invitation Concert . . . Musical Director of the British Broadcasting Corporation . . .' They listened to the normal litany from their normal positions: he aloft in the bed, she in the low basketwork chair, close to the EMG in case the tuning needed adjustment. 'Change to the programme which has been previously announced . . . Glinka . . . new work by the English composer Leonard Verity . . . honour of his seventieth birthday later this year . . . "Four English . . ." '

She howled. He had never heard such a sound emerge from her before. She fought her heavy way downstairs, ignored Marie-Thérèse, and ran out into a wet dark afternoon. Below her, the village jangled with light and flashed with noise: gigantic motors turned and thrummed. A *kermesse* had started in her head with traction engines and flood-lamps, the comic frippery of the roundabout organ, the tinny clatter of the shooting range, the careless blast of cornet and bugle, laughter, fake fear, flashing bulbs, and stupid songs. She ran down the track to the first of these orgiastic sites. The old *boulanger* turned inquisitively as the wild, wet, under-dressed woman irrupted into his son's shop, gave him a mad stare, howled, and ran out again. She, who for years had been so practical, so swift and necessary with the village, now could not even make herself understood. She wanted to strike the whole countryside into silence with fire from the gods. She ran into the butcher's, where Madame was driving her mighty turbine: a throbbing belt, a tormenting scream, blood everywhere. She ran to the nearest farm and saw feed for a hundred thousand cattle being churned and sluiced by a hundred electric pumps. She ran to the American house, but her knocking could not be heard above the antic flushing of a dozen electric water closets. The village was conspiring, just as the world always conspired against the artist, waiting until he was weakest and then seeking to destroy him. The world did it carelessly, without knowing why, without seeing why, just thumbing a switch with a casual clack. And the world didn't even notice, didn't listen, just as now they seemed not to hear the words in her mouth, these faces gathered round, staring at her. He was right, of course he was right, he had always been right. And she had betrayed him in the end, he was right about that, too.

In the kitchen Marie-Thérèse was standing in awkward conspiracy with the curé. Adeline went upstairs to the bedroom and shut the door. He was dead, of course, she knew that. His eyes were closed, either by nature or by human interference. His hair looked as if it had just been combed, and his mouth was turned down in a final sulk. She eased the fire-tongs from his hand, touched his forehead in a spread chord, then lay down on the bed beside him. His body yielded no more in death than it had in life. At last, she fell quiet, and as her senses returned she became loosely aware of Schumann's piano concerto stumbling through the static.

She sent to Paris for a *mouleur*, who took a cast of the composer's face, and one of his right hand. The British Broadcasting Corporation announced the death of Leonard Verity, but since they had so recently given the first performance of his final work, further musical tribute was judged inessential.

Three weeks after the funeral, a square parcel marked 'Fragile' arrived at the house. Adeline was alone. She chipped the sealing-wax from the two fat knots, unfolded layers of corrugated cardboard, and found an obsequious letter from the recording manager. She took each of the 'Four English Seasons' from its stiff manila envelope and sat them on her knee. Idly, methodically, as Leonard would have approved, she ordered them. Spring, Summer, Autumn, Winter. She stared at the edge of the kitchen table, hearing other melodies.

They broke like biscuit. Her thumb bled.

# JUNCTION

$\mathcal{S}$UNDAY WAS FOR hair-cutting and dog-washing. The French party who drove out from Rouen were at first disappointed. Mme Julie had heard tell of gypsies, *banditti*, wandering Israelites and locusts devouring the land. She had enquired of her husband whether they should not carry instruments of protection; but Dr Achille had preferred to rely, for both guidance and possible defence, upon one of his medical students, Charles-André, a sturdy, shy youth born out on the great chalk plain beyond Barentin. The shanty-town, however, proved quiet. Nor was this calm, as they initially suspected, consequent upon the stupefaction of drink, for the men would not be paid until the end of the month, and would only then go on a randy, fighting Jack-come-first, spending their wages in *cabarets* and low taverns, swallowing French brandy as they would English beer, getting drunk and then diligently sustaining that drunkenness so that by the time all had been rounded up the horses at the workface would have been rested a full three days. Rather, what the French party discovered was the calm of orderly repose. A ganger in scarlet plush waistcoat and corduroy breeches was having himself shaved by an itinerant French barber, courteously shifting his short pipe from one side of his mouth to the other in order to facilitate the task. Nearby, a navvy was soaping his lurcher, which whined at the indignity and made as if to bite its master, receiving a hard-palmed cuff in reply. Outside a squat turf shanty, an old witch stood before a stock-pot, into whose grey and turbulent waters a dozen or so thick strings mysteriously disappeared. Each string bore at its dry end a large brown label. Charles-André had heard from one of his fellow students that an English navvy might eat up to five kilogrammes of beef in a normal day. But they were unable to verify this speculation, their nearer approach being discouraged by the witch, who beat her ladle against the stock-pot as if to drive off demons.

———————— o ————————

Yorkey Tom was proud to be a Brassey man. Some of them had been with him from the start, like Bristol Joe and Tenton Punch and Hedgehog and Streaky Bill and Straight-up Nobby. With him since the Chester and Crewe, the London and Southampton, even the Grand Junction. If a navvy fell ill, Mr Brassey supported him until he was fit to work; if one died, he relieved his dependants. Yorkey Tom had seen some deaths in his time. Men crushed by falls of rock, blasters sent to kingdom come by the rash use of gunpowder, boys cut in half under the wheels of soil wagons. When Three-Finger Slen lost his other seven fingers and both forearms too, Mr Brassey paid him forty pounds, and would have paid sixty had Three-Finger not been drunk at the time and nudged the brake with his own shoulder. Mr Brassey was mild in his manner but firm in his decisions. He paid good wages for good work; he knew that ill-paid men took things slow and worked to a lower standard; he also recognised weakness where he saw it, and wouldn't allow tommy-shops, or let travelling beer-sellers trade amongst his men.

Mr Brassey had helped them through that devil's winter three years ago. Hungry navvies crowding the boulevards of Rouen; work on the line from Paris stalled, and nothing on offer back in England. Charity and soup kitchens had kept them alive. It was so cold that the game had gone to ground; Streaky Bill's lurcher scared up hardly a hare all winter. That was when young Mr Brassey the contractor's son had come out to witness the excavations and seen nothing but starving navvies on the idle. His father had forcefully and often repeated the opinion that philanthropy was no substitute for brisk work.

And they had had brisk work in the main, ever since the spring of 1841 when they'd started the 82 miles from Paris to Rouen. Five thousand British labourers brought out by Mr Brassey and Mr Mackenzie had proved insufficient; the contractors had been obliged to hire a second army of Continentals, another five thousand: French, Belgians, Piedmontese, Poles, Dutch, Spaniards. Yorkey Tom had helped train them up. Taught them to eat beef. Taught them what was expected. Rainbow Ratty had the best method: used to line them up, point at the work to be done, stamp his feet and shout *D--n*.

Now he was being examined by Mossoo Frog and his Madame and a boy who trailed behind, peeking and peering. Well, let them look. Let them see how carefully Mossoo Barber went with his razor: everyone knew what had happened when Pigtail Punch was made to bleed by a clumsy cut. Now they were commenting on his Johnny Prescott and his breeches, as if he were some specimen in the zoological gardens. Perhaps he should growl and bare his teeth, stamp his feet and cry *D--n*.

———————— o ————————

The curé of Pavilly was enthusiastic in his faith, protective of his flock, and privately disappointed with the tolerant worldliness of his bishop. The curé was ten years younger than the century, and had been a seminarist during the heretical and blasphemous events of Ménilmontant; later, he had experienced joyful relief at the trial of 1832 and the breaking-up of the sect. Although his current parishioners had little understanding of the intricacies of Saint-Simonisme – not even the pretentious Mlle Delisle, who had once received a letter from Mme Sand – the priest found it useful in his sermons to allude to the *Nouveau Christianisme* and to the diabolic behaviour of the followers of Enfantin. They provided him with helpful and chastening examples of the ubiquity of evil. He was not one of those who, in their observation of the world, confused ignorance with purity of spirit; he knew that temptations were put on earth to strengthen true belief. But he also knew that some, when faced with temptation, would endanger their souls and fall; and in his private solitude he anguished for those sinners, both present and future.

As the Rouen and Le Havre Railway began to scrabble its north-westerly curve from Le Houlme towards Barentin, as the encampments moved nearer, as livestock began to go missing, as the devil's army drew nearer, the curé of Pavilly became troubled.

———————— o ————————

The *Fanal de Rouen*, which liked to take an historical perspective on contemporary events, knowingly observed that this was not the first time that *les Rosbifs* had facilitated progress in the nation's transport system: the first road between Lyon and Clermont-Ferrand had been laid down by British captives under the Emperor Claudius in AD 45–46. The newspaper then offered a comparison between the year 1418, when the city had for months heroically resisted the onslaught of the English King Henry V and his fearful Goddons, and the year 1842, when it had succumbed without a struggle to the mighty army of Mister Thomas Brassey, whose warriors carried picks and shovels across their shoulders in place of the fabled longbow. Finally, the *Fanal* reported, without coming to its own judgment on the matter, that some authorities likened the building of the European railways to the construction of the great medieval cathedrals. The English engineers and contractors, according to such writers, resembled those wandering bands of Italian craftsmen under whose guidance local workmen had erected their own glorious monuments to God.

'That fellow there', said Charles-André when they were out of earshot of the English ganger, 'is capable of shovelling twenty tons of earth in one day. Lifting it above the height of his own head and into a wagon. Twenty tons!'

'Assuredly a monster,' Mme Julie responded. 'And with the diet of a monster.' She shook her pretty head, and the student watched her ringlets tremble like the crystal drops of a chandelier moved by the breeze. Dr Achille, a tall, long-nosed man with the bright vigorous beard of early middle-age, indulgently corrected the fancies of his wife: 'Then look at the sumptuous residence of the Minotaur and his companions.' He pointed to a series of verminous, troglodytic holes gouged directly from the side of the hill. Scarcely superior were the turf shanties, long communal huts and rude wooden sheds which they passed. From one of these dwellings voices were heard in argument, amid them a woman's.

'I understand that their wedding ceremony is most picturesque,' Charles-André remarked. 'The happy couple are made to jump over a broomstick. That is all. Then they are adjudged to be married.'

'Easily done,' said Mme Julie.

'And easily undone,' continued the student. He aspired to sophistication, and was keen to please the doctor's wife, though afraid to shock. 'I was told . . . it is said that they sell their women when they are done with them. They sell them . . . often . . . it seems . . . for a gallon of beer.'

'A gallon of *English* beer?' enquired the doctor, setting the student at his ease by a levity of manner. 'Now that really is too low a price.' His wife struck him playfully on the arm. 'I would not sell *you*, my dear, for anything less than a tonneau of the finest Bordeaux,' he continued, and was struck again, to his pleasure. Charles-André was envious of such intimacy.

———— o ————

In constructing the 82 miles of the Paris and Rouen Railway Mr Joseph Locke the Engineer was able merely to follow the leisurely descent of the River Seine between those two great cities. But in extending the line to Le Havre – where it would connect with steamer services across the English Channel, and thence with the London and Southampton Railway, completing the route from Paris to London – he was confronted by more strenuous feats of engineering. These difficulties were reflected in the tender price: £15,700 per mile for the Paris and Rouen, in excess of £23,000 per mile for the additional 58 miles of the Rouen and Le Havre. Moreover, the French government insisted upon an investigation into the proposed gradients of the line. Mr Locke had initially proposed a maximum of 1 in 110. Some of the French argued for 1 in 200 on grounds of safety, a proposal which would either have imposed a considerably longer route, or else caused much additional cutting and embanking, thus greatly increasing the cost. Eventually, a compromise gradient of 1 in 125 was agreed between the parties.

Mr Brassey had established himself at Rouen once more, this time accompanied by his wife Maria, who spoke the French language fluently and was able to act as interpreter with officials from the French Ministry. They paid their respects to the Consul, and made themselves known at the Anglican church of All Saints on the Ile Lacroix. They enquired about a circulating library of English books, but none had yet been established. In her idle moments Mrs Brassey visited the great Gothic edifices of the city: St-Ouen, with its lofty triforium and glittering rose-window; St-Maclou, with its carved doors and grotesque Last Judgment; and the Cathedral of Notre-Dame, where a verger in full regalia, with plumed hat, rapier and staff, imposed his presence upon her. He pointed out the circumference of the Amboise bell, the resting place of Pierre de Brézé, the effigy of Diane de Poitiers and a mutilated statue from the tomb of Richard Coeur-de-Lion. He indicated the Gargoyle Window, and recounted the legend of the Tour de Beurre, erected in the seventeenth century with money paid for indulgences to eat butter during Lent.

Mr Brassey's men took the line from the terminus of the Paris and Rouen, swung it across the Seine on a new bridge, then bent it in a northerly loop through the hills and valleys of the city. They built the Ste-Catherine Tunnel, 1600 metres in length; raised the Darnétal Viaduct; blasted out the tunnels of Beauvoisine, St-Maur and Mont Riboudet. They traversed the river Cailly just south of Malaunay. Ahead lay the river Austreberthe, which was to be crossed at Barentin by a fine and elegant viaduct. Mrs Brassey informed her husband about the Tour de Beurre, and wondered what edifices could be raised in their own day from the sale of indulgences.

———————  o  ———————

'Prepare ye the way of the Lord, make straight in the desert a highway for our God. Every valley shall be exalted, and every mountain and hill shall be made low: and the crooked shall be made straight, and the rough places plain.' The assembled villagers of Pavilly duly expected an appeal for willing hands to improve the ragged path which ran from the church to the cemetery. But there seemed no immediate connection between the curé's introductory citation from the Book of Isaiah and his subsequent comments. He began to warn his flock, and not for the first time, against the perils of a doctrine few had heard of and fewer still would have been tempted by. The farmer who kept the land at Les Pucelles stirred impatiently at the priest's educated style. In the back pew Adèle, who had been worked harder than usual by her mistress that week, yawned openly.

The curé explained how those heresies most dangerous to Christian doctrine were the very ones which seem to propose themselves as an agreeable and seductive version of the true faith: such was the Devil's way. The Comte de Saint-Simon, for instance, had affirmed, among other matters, that society must strive towards the amelioration of the moral and physical existence of the poorest class. Such an idea was not strange to those familiar with the teachings of Our Lord in his Sermon on the Mount. And yet what, upon closer examination, did the heretic actually intend? That the direction of society, of Christian society, be handed over to men of science and to the industrial chieftains! That the spiritual leadership of the world be taken from the Holy Father in Rome and transferred to the makers of machines!

And how, moreover, had the followers of this false prophet comported themselves when they banded together into a sinful community to pursue the iniquitous principles of their late leader? They had publicly espoused the community of goods, abolition of the right of inheritance, and the enfranchisement of women. All of which meant that unmarried people of opposite sex lived communally like the brute polygamists of the East; even as they proclaimed the equality of woman with man, they brazenly practised prostitution. The curé of Pavilly spared his listeners the theory of the rehabilitation of the flesh, which he himself knew without examination to be blasphemous, and warned them instead about the dangers attendant upon peculiar and eccentric dress. Those who set themselves up against the true authority of God's word frequently chose to mark themselves out by adopting a uniform. Thus in the communistic society of Ménilmontant they had worn white trousers to symbolise love, a red waistcoat to symbolise work, and a blue tunic to symbolise faith. This last garment was tailored so that it buttoned at the back, a particular which the polygamists asserted as proof of their fraternity, since none could put on his tunic without the assistance of another. The curé at this point left a passage of holy silence, during which some of his congregation correctly guessed at what he felt unable to express: that the polygamists were therefore also incapable of undressing themselves without assistance.

Adèle in the back pew was by now fully attentive, gazing at the buttons on the front of the priest's cassock as if gazing at virtue itself; while at the same time remembering a scarlet plush waistcoat which she had set eyes upon only a few days previously. The curé announced his intention of returning to this same theme the following Sunday, and began the blessing.

———————— o ————————

The French party walked on as far as the cutting. Given the notorious godlessness of the English navvies, they had the vivid expectation of at least seeing a few men labouring blasphemously on the Sabbath; but all remained quiet. The slashed earth peacefully displayed its thick stripes of white chalk, yellow gravel and orange clay. Dr Achille admired the neatness of the incision these rough men had made in the planet's skin.

Within the chalky ravine the barrow runs were deserted. Charles-André, who was an amateur of the excavations, tried to explain their manner of operation: the planking laid up the sharp slope, the pole at the top of the embankment, the pulley atop the pole, the horse attached to the rope to help the navvy propel his full barrow up the hillside. Charles-André had witnessed immense loads being raised by this method; he had also seen mud sluicing down wet planks, a panicky horse unable to keep its feet, and a navvy hurling himself aside to avoid being crushed by his own barrow. Only the strongest fellows, the giants of the enterprise, had the fortitude and the audacity to perform such labour.

'Five kilos of beef,' observed Dr Achille.

'Even so,' said Mme Julie, reflecting on the considerable dangers of the enterprise, 'you would think, would you not, that with ingenuity, surely a machine might raise the earth instead?'

'There was one invented, I understand. A moving platform. The navvies judged it a threat to their wages, and destroyed it.'

'I am glad they are not saints,' rejoined Achille.

As they strolled back towards the encampment, they heard a language not their own, yet not a foreign tongue either. Two men were repairing a shovel, whose shaft was loose on its blade. The larger fellow giving instruction was an English ganger, and the smaller one, owner of the shovel, a French peasant. Their patois, or *lingua franca*, was partly English, partly French, and the rest an *olla podrida* of other languages. Even those words familiar to the listeners, however, were forced into a distorted shape; while grammar was wrenched violently out of its true way. Yet the repairers of the shovel, fluent in this macaronic, understood one another perfectly.

'That is how we shall talk in the future,' claimed the student with sudden confidence. 'No more misapprehensions. Nations shall mend their differences as these two fellows are mending their shovel.'

'No more poetry,' said Mme Julie with a sigh.

'No more wars,' countered Charles-André.

'Nonsense,' Dr Achille responded. 'Merely different poetry, different wars.'

———————— ○ ————————

The curé of Pavilly returned to Chapter XL of the Book of Isaiah. Adèle stared at the priest's virtuous buttons, but he had no more to say about the significance of dress. Instead, he began to explain how the trial and condemnation of the polygamists at Ménilmontant for actions prejudicial to the social order had severed one head of the hydra, but how others had grown in its place. That which heretical doctrine had failed to achieve was to be attained instead by engineering. It was known that many members of the disbanded sect were now active as scientists and engineers, spreading like a canker through the body of France. Some of their number had for years proposed the building of a canal at the Isthmus of Suez. Then there was the Jew Pereire, who openly proclaimed the Railway an instrument of civilisation. Blasphemous comparisons had been made with those holy artisans who had constructed the great cathedrals. The curé protested: the truer analogy was with the heathen Pyramid-builders of ancient Egypt. The English engineers and their ungodly navvies came merely to erect the new follies of the modern age, to manifest once more the vanity of Man in his worship of false gods.

He did not mean that such road building was in itself contrary to the Christian faith. But if the valleys were to be exalted, the mountains and hills to be made low, if the crooked were to be made straight and the rough places plain as had been done with the crossing of the river Cailly near Malaunay and with the proposed viaduct at Barentin, then such deeds must occur, as Isaiah instructed, in order to prepare the way of the Lord, to make a highway in the desert for God. Unless Man's purpose was guided by the greater purpose of God's law, then Man remained a brute beast and his greatest labours amounted to no more than the sin of pride.

In the back row, Adèle dozed. The farmer who kept the

land at Les Pucelles, having profited well from the appropriation of land required by the Rouen and Le Havre Railway, and having also contributed publicly to the Diocesan Relief Fund for Orphans and Widows, complained in writing to the Bishop about the young priest's tendency to theoretical fulmination. What the parish needed was straightforward moral instruction on matters of local interest and concern. The Bishop duly admonished the curé of Pavilly, while simultaneously congratulating himself on his astuteness in placing the young man at a safe distance from the city. Let him burn out his fire and his wrath among simple souls, where little harm would be done. The Church was a place for faith, not ideas.

———————— ○ ————————

The French party made their way back to the first huts of the shanty village.

'So we have not been attacked by banditti?' Achille observed.

'Not yet,' replied his wife.

'Nor robbed by gypsies?'

'No.'

'Nor bitten by a plague of locusts?'

'Not exactly.'

'Nor seen the Pyramid slaves whipped?'

She struck him skittishly on the arm, and he smiled.

The navvy who had been soaping his lurcher was gone. 'Those dogs are trained to kill our game,' complained Charles-André. 'Two of them can take down a fully grown sheep, they say.'

But Dr Achille's good humour could not be shifted.

'There are enough rabbits in our country. I would exchange a railway for a few rabbits.'

Yorkey Tom was sitting on the same hard little chair as before, warming his newly shaven chin in the sun. The short pipe clamped in the corner of his mouth pointed nearly to the vertical, and his eyes appeared tight shut. Cautiously, the French party re-examined this ferocious consumer of beef, this lusty scavenger. The ganger had adopted nothing of the French way of dressing. He wore a velvet square-tailed coat, a scarlet plush waistcoat patterned with small black spots, and corduroy breeches held by a leather strap at the waist with further straps at the knee, below which swelling calves descended to a pair of thick high-low boots. Beside him, upon a stool, lay a white felt hat with the brim turned up. He appeared exotic yet sturdy, a strange but commonsensical beast. He was also quite content to be observed, for the eyelid he kept quarter-open to guard his hat also gave him a view of these gawping frog-eaters.

They were at least politely keeping their distance. He had been in France for the best part of five years, and during that time he had been poked and prodded, gazed at and spat upon; dogs had been set on him and local bullies had mistakenly shown a desire to try their strength. Against this, he had also been applauded, bussed, embraced, fed and fêted. In many parts the local Frenchies regarded the excavations as a kind of free entertainment, and the English navvies would sometimes respond by putting on a show of how hard they could work. Ginger Billy, who had taken a Frenchwoman to wife for a couple of years on the Paris and Rouen, would translate their varied expressions of amazement, which Yorkey Tom and his gang took pleasure in provoking. They were kings of their work, and they knew so. It took a year to harden up a healthy English farm labourer into a navvy, and the transformation was even greater for a French spindle-shank who ate only bread, vegetables and fruit, who needed frequent rest and a supply of kerchiefs to mop his poor face.

Now the French party's attention was distracted by an argument from the neighbouring shanty. The old witch was heaving at one of the thick strings which disappeared into the mire and filth of her stock-pot. Beside her stood a growl-ing, bearded giant, suspiciously checking the hieroglyph on the end of the cable. Up came a joint of submerged meat, the string piercing its centre. The crone tossed it on to a plate and added a wedge of bread. The hairy navvy now transferred his suspicion from the label to the viand. In its few hours under the guardianship of the old woman, it seemed to have lost some of its shape, much of its colour, and all of its identity. The giant began to berate her, though whether for her cooking or for her lack of honesty it was impossible to tell; though both parties were English, their bellowing and screeching were conducted in the excluding *lingua franca* of the encampments.

Still smiling at this comedy, the French party returned to their carriage.

———————— o ————————

The curé of Pavilly, brought to order by his bishop, left the realm of the theoretical. It was his duty to warn his parish-ioners in the sternest of terms against contact with the approaching army of Philistines and Barbarians. He had con-ducted an investigation, even going among them himself, and had obtained the following intelligence. First, that they were Christians neither in the observance of the faith nor in their moral behaviour. As proof of this, they had rejected their names of Christian baptism, preferring to make themselves known by false names, no doubt with the intention of misleading the forces of order. They did not observe the Sabbath, either working upon the holy day, or else reserving it for activities which ranged from the frivolous, like the washing of their dogs, to the criminal, as in the use of the same dogs for the theft of game and livestock. It was true that they worked hard, and were justly rewarded for their labours, but their threefold wages merely thrust them three times deeper into brutishness. Nor had they any sense of thrift, spending their money as they got it, preferably upon drink. They thieved with no attempt at concealment. Further, they flouted the laws of Christian marriage, living with women in an open state of fornication, and even denying such women the least modesty; their communal huts amounted to no more than dens of prostitution. Those who spoke their own native language blasphemed constantly in the course of their labour; while those who spoke the common language of the excavations were no better than the builders of the Tower of Babel – and did not the Tower remain unfinished and its builders confounded and scattered upon the face of the earth? Finally and greatly, the navvies were blasphemers by their very deeds, since they exalted the valleys and made the rough places plain for their own purposes, heedless and scornful of the purposes of the Lord.

The farmer who kept the fields at Les Pucelles nodded approvingly at the priest. What did you come to church for, if not to hear a powerful denunciation of others and an implicit confirmation of your own virtue? The girl Adèle in the back pew had also been attending carefully, her mouth falling open on occasion.

The French party, who had become regular gawpers at the excavations, who had marvelled at the skills and scorned dangers of the barrow-run, and had come to comprehend why an English navvy was paid 3s 6d to 3s 9d per diem while his French counterpart received 1s 8d to 2s 3d, visited the railway workings for the last time towards the end of the year 1845. The Viaduct at Barentin was now almost complete. Across frosted fields they viewed the structure: 100 feet high, one third of a mile long, with twenty-seven arches each boasting a span of 50 feet. It had cost, Charles-André assured them, some fifty thousand English pounds, and was soon to be inspected by the Minister of Public Works and other high French officials.

Dr Achille examined the slow curve of the Viaduct as it crossed the valley floor, and counted off to himself the elegant, symmetrical arches. 'I cannot think,' he said at last, 'why my brother, who claims to be an artist, cannot see the immense beauty of the railways. Why should he dislike them so intensely? He is too young to be so old-fashioned.'

'He maintains, I believe,' replied Mme Julie with some care, 'that scientific advances make us blind to moral defects. They give us the illusion that we are making progress, which he contends to be dangerous. At least, this is what he says,' she added, as if in qualification.

'That fits his character,' said her husband. 'Too clever to see the simple truth. Look at that edifice before us. A surgeon may now travel more quickly to save a patient's leg. Where is the illusion in that?'

In the first days of January 1846, shortly after the approving visit of the French Minister of Public Works, torrential rain fell in the region north of Rouen. At approximately six o'clock in the morning of January 10th, the fifth arch of the Barentin Viaduct sundered and fell. One by one the other arches followed, until the entire structure lay in ruins upon the sodden valley floor. Whether the fault lay in over-hasty construction, inadequate local lime, or the tempestuous conditions, remained unclear; but the French newspapers, among them the *Fanal de Rouen*, encouraged a xenophobic response to the calamity. Not only were Mr Locke the Engineer, and Mr Brassey and Mr Mackenzie the contractors, all three of them English, but so were most of the labourers, and also most of the investors in the project. What interest could they have except that of extracting money from France while leaving behind faulty workmanship?

The curé of Pavilly felt himself vindicated. The Tower of Babel had fallen and the workmen were confounded. Those who had blasphemed by calling themselves the new cathedral builders had been cast down. The Lord had demonstrated his disapproval. Let them build their folly up again, howsoever high they liked, for nothing could now erase the divine gesture. The sin of pride had been punished; but lest he himself be tempted towards that same path, the priest devoted his sermon the following Sunday to the duty of charity. The farmer who kept the fields at Les Pucelles contributed more generously than usual to the collection. The girl Adèle was missing from the rear pew. She had been absent from the village many times in recent weeks, and her vocabulary had become infected with strange half-bred words. Not everyone was surprised in Pavilly; her mistress had often remarked that Adèle was likely to become fat before she became honest.

Mr Brassey and Mr Mackenzie were greatly distressed by the misfortune at Barentin, but responded manfully. They waited for neither litigation nor the apportionment of blame, commencing at once the search for several million new bricks. Suspecting local lime to be the cause of the disaster, they brought in hydraulic lime from a distance away. With energy and determination, and with the skill of their agents, Mr Brassey and Mr Mackenzie succeeded in rebuilding the Viaduct in less than six months, the whole expense of which they bore themselves.

———————— ○ ————————

The curé of Pavilly did not attend the opening ceremony of the Rouen and Le Havre Railway. There was a military guard of honour, and good society of both sexes, including Dr Achille and Mme Julie, was present. Priests in winged surplices bore aloft stout candles which reached the height of the locomotive's steam dome. As Mr Locke the Engineer and his two contractors doffed their hats, the Bishop passed alongside the sleek cylindrical engine built by Mr William Buddicom, formerly Superintendent at Crewe, in his new works at Sotteville. The Bishop sprinkled holy water upon the fire box, the boiler and the smoke box; he cast it upwards at the steam-cock and the safety valves; then, as if not satisfied, he retraced his steps and asperged the driving wheels, the crank axle and the connecting rods, the buffers and the chimney and the starting handle and the foot-board. Nor did he forget the tender, in which several high dignitaries were already seated. He attended to the connecting links, the water tank and the spring buffers; he doused the brake as if he were Saint Christopher himself. The locomotive engine was entirely blessed, its journeys and its purposes placed under the protection of God and his saints.

Later, there was a feast for the English navvies. The French cavalry stood guard while several oxen were roasted and the labourers drank their fill. They remained good-natured despite intoxication, and afterwards danced vigorously, directing their partners with the firm dexterity they daily used upon their barrows. Adèle was swung between Yorkey Tom and Straight-up Nobby. When it grew dark they set off fog signals in celebration of the day, and the sudden noise caused alarm among the fearful. The *Fanal de Rouen* reported the event at length, and while recalling once more the downfall of the Viaduct at Barentin, praised the Homeric stature of the English navvies and, in a benign confusion of cultures, likened them one last time to the builders of the great cathedrals.

Ten years after the opening of the Rouen and Le Havre Railway, Thomas Brassey was officially rewarded for his many labours in France. By this time he had also built the Orléans and Bordeaux Railway, the Amiens and Boulogne, the Rouen and Dieppe, the Nantes and Caen, the Caen and Cherbourg. The Emperor Napoleon III invited him to a dinner at the Tuileries. The contractor sat near to the Empress, and was especially moved by her kindness in talking English to him for the greater part of the time. In the course of the evening the Emperor of the French ceremoniously invested Mr Brassey with the Cross of the Légion d'honneur. Upon receiving this insigne, the foreign contractor replied modestly, 'Mrs Brassey will be pleased to have it.'

# EXPERIMENT

HIS STORY didn't always begin in the same way. In the preferred version, my Uncle Freddy was in Paris on business, travelling for a firm which produced authentic wax polish. He went into a bar and ordered a glass of white wine. The man standing next to him asked what his area of activity was, and he replied, 'Cire réaliste.'

But I also heard my uncle tell it differently. For instance, he had been taken to Paris by a rich patron to act as navigator in a motor rally. The stranger in the bar (we are now at The Ritz, by the way) was refined and haughty, so my uncle's French duly rose to the occasion. Asked his purpose in the city, he replied, 'Je suis, sire, rallyiste.' In a third, and it seemed to me most implausible version – but then the quotidian is often preposterous, and so the preposterous may in return be plausible – the white wine in front of my uncle was a Reuilly. This, he would explain, came from a small appellation in the Loire, and was not unlike Sancerre in style. My uncle was new to Paris, and had already ingested several glasses (the location having shifted to a *petit zinc* in the *quartier Latin*), so that when the stranger (who this time was not haughty) asked what he was drinking, he felt that panic when a foreign idiom escapes the mind, and the further panic as an English phrase is desperately translated. The idiomatic model he chose was 'I'm on the beer', and so he said, 'Je suis sur Reuillys.' Once, when I rebuked my uncle for the contradictoriness of his memories, he gave a contented little smile. 'Marvellous, the subconscious, isn't it?' he replied. 'So inventive.'

If the neighbouring drinker came in several physical forms, he likewise introduced himself variously as Tanguy, Prévert, Duhamel and Unik; once even as Breton himself. We can, at least, be sure of the date of this untrustworthy encounter: March 1928. Further, my Uncle Freddy, as even the most cautious commentators have agreed, is – was – none other than the mildly disguised 'T.F.', who appears in Session 5(a) of the Surrealist Group's famously unplatonic dialogues about sex. The transcript of this session was published as an appendix to *Recherches sur la sexualité, janvier 1928 – août 1932*. The notes state that my uncle was almost certainly introduced to the group by Pierre Unik, and that 'T.F.', contrary to the subsequent meanderings of his subconscious, was actually in Paris on holiday.

We shouldn't be too sceptical about my uncle's undeserved *entrée* to the Surrealist circle. They did, after all, admit occasional outsiders – an unfrocked priest, a Communist Party militant – to their discussions. And perhaps they thought a conventional twenty-nine-year-old Englishman supposedly acquired through a linguistic misunderstanding might usefully broaden their terms of reference. My uncle was fond of attributing his permitted presence to the French dictum that within every lawyer there lurk the remnants of a poet. I am not of either world, you understand (and neither was my uncle). Is this piece of wisdom any truer than its opposite: that within every poet there lurk the remnants of a lawyer?

Uncle Freddy maintained that the session which he

attended took place in the apartment of the man he met in the bar; which limits it to five possible locations. There were about a dozen participants according to my uncle; nine according to the *Recherches*. I should make it clear that since Session 5(a) was not published until 1990, and my uncle died in 1985, he was only ever faced with self-inflicted incompatibilities. Further, the tale of Uncle Freddy and the Surrealists was strictly for what he called the smoking-room, where narrative libertarianism was more acceptable. After swearing listeners to lifelong silence *vis-à-vis* Aunt Kate, he would enlarge on the frank licentiousness of what had taken place back in 1928. At times he would claim to have been shocked, and maintain that he had heard more filth in one evening among Parisian intellectuals than he had in three years of barrack-room life during the last war. At others, his self-presentation was as the English man-about-town, the card, the dandy, all too willing to pass on a few tips, a few handy refinements of technique, to this gathering of Frenchmen whose cerebral intensity, in his view, hampered their normal sensual responses.

The published Session, needless to say, confirms neither version. Those who have read the *Recherches* will be familiar with their strange mixture of pseudo-scientific inquiry and frank subjective response. The truth is that everyone talks about sex in a different way, just as everyone, we naturally assume, does it in a different way. André Breton, animator of the group, is a lofty Socratic figure, austere and at times repellent ('I don't like anyone to caress me. I hate that.'). The others are variously benign to cynical, self-mocking to boastful, candid to satirical. The dialogues are happily full of humour; occasionally of the unintended sort, inflicted by posterity's frigid judgment; but more often intended, issuing from a rueful acknowledgment of our human frailty. For instance, in Session 3, Breton is catechising his male companions about whether they would allow a woman to touch their sex when it was not erect. Marcel Noll replies that he hates it. Benjamin Péret says that if a woman does that to him, he feels diminished. Breton agrees: diminished is exactly the right word for how he would feel. To which Louis Aragon rejoins: 'If a woman touched my sex only when it was erect, it wouldn't get that way very often.'

I am straying from the point. I'm probably also trying to put off the admission that my uncle's participation in Session 5(a) is for most of its extent frankly disappointing. Perhaps there was a false democracy in the assumption that an Englishman picked up in a bar because of a verbal mistake would have important testimony to offer this probing tribunal. 'T.F.' is asked many of the usual questions: under what conditions he prefers to have sex; how he lost his virginity; whether and how he can tell if a woman has reached orgasm; how many people he has had sexual relations with; how recently he has masturbated; how many times in succession he is capable of orgasm; and so on. I shall not bother to relate my uncle's responses, because they are either banal or, I suspect, not wholly truthful. When asked by Breton the characteristically compendious question, 'Apart from ejaculating in the vagina, mouth or anus, where do you like to ejaculate in order of preference: 1) Armpit; 2) Between the breasts; 3) On the stomach?' Uncle Freddy answers – and here I have to retranslate from the French, so do not offer these as his exact words – 'Is the cupped palm permitted?' Quizzed about which sexual position he prefers, my uncle replies that he likes to be lying on his back, with the woman sitting on top of him. 'Ah,' says Benjamin Péret, 'the so-called "lazy position".'

My uncle is then interrogated about the British propensity

for sodomy, over which he is defensive, until it transpires that homosexuality is not the topic, but rather sodomy between men and women. Then my uncle is baffled. 'I have never done it,' he replies, 'and I have never heard of anyone doing it.' 'But do you dream of doing it?' asks Breton. 'I have never dreamed of doing it,' 'T.F.' doggedly responds. 'Have you ever dreamed of fucking a nun in a church?' is Breton's next question. 'No, never.' 'What about a priest or a monk?' asks Queneau. 'No, not that either,' is the reply.

I am not surprised that Session 5(a) is relegated to an appendix. The interrogators and fellow-confessors are in a lethargic or routine mood; while the surprise witness keeps pleading the Fifth. Then, towards the end of the evening, there comes a moment when the Englishman's presence seems briefly justified. I feel I should at this point give the transcript in full.

ANDRE BRETON: What is your opinion of love?

'T.F.': When two people get married . . .

ANDRE BRETON: No, no, no! The word *marriage* is anti-surrealist.

JEAN BALDENSPERGER: What about sexual relations with animals?

'T.F.': What do you mean?

JEAN BALDENSPERGER: Sheep. Donkeys.

'T.F.': There are very few donkeys in Ealing. We had a pet rabbit.

JEAN BALDENSPERGER: Did you have relations with the rabbit?

'T.F.': No.

JEAN BALDENSPERGER: Did you dream of having relations with the rabbit?

'T.F.': No.

ANDRE BRETON: I cannot believe that your sexual life can possibly be as empty of imagination and surrealism as you make it appear.

JACQUES PREVERT: Can you describe to us the principal differences between sexual relations with an Englishwoman and those with a Frenchwoman?

'T.F.': I only arrived in France yesterday.

JACQUES PREVERT: Are you frigid? No, do not take offence. I am not serious.

'T.F.': Perhaps I can make a contribution by describing something I used to dream about.

JEAN BALDENSPERGER: To do with donkeys?

'T.F.': No. There used to be a pair of twin sisters in my street.

JEAN BALDENSPERGER: You wanted to have sexual relations with both of them at the same time?

RAYMOND QUENEAU: How old were they? Were they young girls?

PIERRE UNIK: You are excited by lesbianism? You like to watch women caress one another?

ANDRE BRETON: Please, gentlemen, let our guest speak. I know we are surrealists, but this is chaos.

'T.F.': I used to look at these twin sisters, who were in all visible respects identical, and ask how far that identity continued.

ANDRE BRETON: You mean, if you were having sexual relations with one, how could you tell it was she and not the other?

'T.F.': Exactly. At the beginning. And this in turn provoked a further question. What if there were two people – women – who in their . . .

ANDRE BRETON: In their sexual movements . . .

'T.F.': In their sexual movements were exactly the same, and yet in all other respects were completely different.

PIERRE UNIK: Erotic doppelgangers yet social disparates.

ANDRE BRETON: Precisely. That is a valuable contribution. Even, if I may say so to our English guest, a quasi-surrealist contribution.

JACQUES PREVERT: So you have not yet been in bed with a Frenchwoman?

'T.F.': I told you, I only arrived yesterday.

This is the end of Uncle Freddy's documented participation in Session 5(a), which then returned to matters previously discussed in Session 3, namely the distinction between orgasm and ejaculation, and the relation between dreams and masturbatory desire. My uncle evidently had little to contribute on these subjects.

I had, of course, no suspicion of this future corroboration when I saw my uncle for the last time. This was in November of 1984. Aunt Kate was dead by now, and my visits to 'T.F.' (as I am inclined to think of him nowadays) had become increasingly dutiful. Nephews tend to prefer aunts to uncles. Aunt Kate was dreamy and indulgent; there was something gauzy-scarved and secretive about her. Uncle Freddy was indecently foursquare; he seemed to have his thumbs in his waistcoat pockets even when wearing a two-piece suit. His stance, both moral and physical, had the bullying implication that he truly understood what manhood consisted of, that his generation had miraculously caught the elusive balance between earlier repression and subsequent laxness, and that any deviation from this *beau idéal* was regrettable, if not actively perverse. As a result, I was never quite at ease with the future 'T.F.'. He once announced that it was his avuncular responsibility to teach me about wine, but his pedantry and assertiveness put me off the subject until quite recently.

It had become a routine after Aunt Kate's death that I would take Uncle Freddy out to dinner on his birthday, and that afterwards we would return to his flat off the Cromwell Road and drink ourselves stupid. The consequences mattered little to him; but I had my patients to think of, and would annually try to avoid getting as drunk as I had the previous year. I can't say I ever succeeded, because though each year my resolution was stronger, so was the countervailing force of my uncle's tediousness. In my experience, there are various good but lesser motives – guilt, fear, misery, happiness – for indulging in a certain excess of drink, and one larger motive for indulging in a great excess: boredom. At one time I knew a clever alcoholic who insisted that he drank because things then happened to him such as never did when he was sober. I half-believed him, though to my mind drink does not really make things happen, it simply helps you bear the pain of things not happening. For instance, the pain of my uncle being exceptionally boring on his birthdays.

The ice would fissure as it hit the whisky, the casing of the gas-fire would clunk, Uncle Freddy would light what he claimed was his annual cigar, and the conversation would turn yet again to what I now think of as Session 5(a).

'So remind me, Uncle, what you were really doing in Paris.'

'Trying to make ends meet. What all young men do.' We were on our second half-bottle of whisky; a third would be required before a welcome enough form of anaesthesia developed. 'Task of the male throughout history, wouldn't you say?'

'And did you?'

'Did I what?'

'Make ends meet?'

'You've a filthy mind for one of your age,' he said, with the sudden sideways aggression that liquor imparts.

'Chip off the old block, Uncle Freddy.' I didn't, of course, mean it.

'Did I ever tell you . . .' and he was launched, if that verb doesn't give too vivid an impression of directness and purpose. This time he had again chosen to be in Paris as map-reader and mechanic to some English milord.

'What sort of car was it? Just out of interest.'

'Panhard,' he answered sniffily. It always was a Panhard when he told this version. I used to divert myself by wondering whether such consistency on my uncle's part made this element of his story more likely to be true, or more likely to be false.

'And where did the rally go?'

'Up hill and down dale, my boy. Round and about. From one end of the land to the other.'

'Trying to make ends meet.'

'Wash your mouth out.'

'Chip off the old . . .'

'So I was in this bar . . .'

I caressed him with the questions he needed, until he reached the normal climax to his story, which was one of the few points at which he agreed with the subsequently published Session 5(a).

'. . . so Fellow-me-lad says to me, "Have you done it with a French lass yet?" and I say, "Give us time, only got off the boat yesterday!" '

I would normally have feigned a run of dying chuckles, poured some more Scotch, and waited for Uncle Freddy's next topic. This time, for some reason, I declined his ending.

'So did you?'

'Did I what?'

'Do it with a French lass?'

I was breaking the rules, and his reply was a kind of rebuke; or at least, I took it as such. 'Your Aunt Kate was as pure as driven snow,' he announced with a hiccup. 'The missing doesn't get any the less, you know, for all the years. I can't wait to join her.'

'Never say die, Uncle Freddy.' This is not the sort of expression I normally use. I practically added, 'Life in the old dog yet', such was the infectious, indeed pestiferous influence of my uncle. Instead, I repeated 'So did you do it with a French lass?'

'Thereby hangs a tale, my boy, and it's one I've never told a living soul.'

I think if I'd shown genuine interest at this point, I might have scared him off, but I was slumped in the oppressive reflection that my uncle was not just an old bore, but a parody of an old bore. Why didn't he strap on a peg-leg and start capering round some inglenooked pub waving a clay pipe? 'Thereby hangs a tale, and it's one I've never told a living soul'. People don't say that any more. Except my uncle just had.

'They fixed me up, you see.'

'Who fixed you up?'

'The Surrealist boys. My new-found chums.'

'You mean, they found you a job?'

'Are you stupid tonight or just normal? I'm not sure I can tell. They fixed me up with a woman. Well, two to be precise.'

I began to pay attention at this point. Needless to say, I did not believe my uncle. He was probably fed up with the lack of impact made by the umpteenth retelling of How I

Met The Surrealists, and had been working up some new embellishment.

'You see, in my considered opinion, those get-togethers . . . They all wanted to meet up and talk smut, but couldn't admit it, so they said there was some scientific purpose behind it all. Fact is, they weren't very good at talking smut. Inhibited, really, I suppose I'd say. Intellectuals. No fire in their veins, just ideas. Why, in my three years in the army . . .'

I will spare you this ritual diversion.

'. . . so I could sense what they were after, but I wasn't going to provide it. Almost like betraying your country, talking smut to a group of foreigners. Unpatriotic, don't you think?'

'Never tried it, Uncle.'

'Ha. You've got a tongue on you tonight. Never tried it. That was just like them, wanting to know what I'd never tried. Trouble with their sort is, if you say you've never wanted to do so-and-so, they don't believe you. In fact, just because you say you *don't* want to do so-and-so, they assume that deep down this is what you're busting to do. Cock-eyed, eh?'

'Could be.'

'So I thought it incumbent upon me to raise the tone of the gathering. Don't laugh, I know what I'm saying. You wait till you find yourself sitting around with a lot of intellectuals all talking about John Thomas. So I said, "Here's one to think about. What if there were two lasses who made love in the same way? Exactly the same way, so that if you closed your eyes you couldn't tell the difference. Wouldn't that be a thing?" I said. And with all their brains they hadn't turned up that conundrum before. It set them by the ears, I don't mind telling you.'

I'm not surprised. It's one of those questions you tend not to ask. Neither about yourself (is there somebody else out there who does it in a way indistinguishable from me?), nor about others. In sex, we observe distinctiveness not similarity. She/he is/was good/not so good/wonderful/bit boring/fakey, or whatever; but we don't as a rule think, oh, being in bed with her was very much like being in bed with so-and-so a couple of years ago. In fact, if I were to close my eyes . . . We don't, on the whole, think that way. Courtesy, in part, I expect; a desire to maintain the individuality of others. And perhaps, a fear that if you do that to them, they might start thinking the same back about you.

'So my new chums fixed me up.'

'. . . ?'

'They wanted to thank me for my contribution to their discussions. Seeing as I'd been so useful. Chappie I'd met in the bar said he'd be in touch.'

'Surely the rally was about to start, Uncle?' Well, it was hard to resist.

'The next day he pitched up and said the group was offering me what he called a Surrealist gift. They were touched by the fact that I had not as yet enjoyed the favours of a French lass, and they were prepared to right this wrong.'

'Remarkably generous.' A remarkable fantasy is what I really thought.

'He said they'd booked a room for me at three o'clock the next afternoon in a hotel off Saint-Sulpice. He said he'd be there too. I thought this a bit strange, but on the other hand, never look a gift-horse and all that. "What are you going to be there for?" I asked. "I don't need my hand holding." So he explained the arrangement. They wanted me to take part in a test. They wanted to know if sex with a Frenchwoman was different from sex with an Englishwoman. I said why did they need me to help them find that out. They said they thought I'd have a more straightforward response. Meaning, I suppose, that I wouldn't sit around and think about it all the time like they would.

'I said, "Let me get this straight. You want me to have a couple of hours with a French lass and then come round the next day and tell you what I thought of it?" "No," Chappie says, "Not the next day, day after. The *next* day we've booked you the same room with another girl." "That's handsome," I say, "two French lasses for the price of one." "Not quite," he says, "one of them is English. You have to tell which is which." "Well," I say, "I can tell that just by saying Bonjour and looking at them." "That's why," he says, "you aren't allowed to say Bonjour and you aren't allowed to look at them. I'll be there when you arrive and blindfold you, then I'll let the girl in. When she's gone and you hear the door shut, you can take the blindfold off. How do you feel about that?"

'How did I feel about that? Well, you could have knocked me down. I'd just been thinking, Don't look a gift-horse in the mouth, and now it was a question of not looking *two* gift-horses in the mouth, or anywhere else. How did I feel? Man to man, I felt like a couple of Christmases had come round at the same time. Part of me wasn't too partial to the blindfold business; though, man to man, another part of me rather was.'

Isn't it pathetic how old men lie about the sex they had in earlier days? What could be more transparently an invention? Paris, youth, a woman, *two* women, a hotel room in the afternoon, all set up and paid for by someone else? Pull the other one, Uncle. Twenty minutes in an *hotel de passe* with a rough hand-towel and a subsequent dose of clap is more like it. Why do old men need this sort of comfort? And what banal scenarios they drool out to themselves. OK, Uncle, fast forward with the soft porn. We'll forget about navigating in the rally.

'So I said count me in. And then next afternoon I went to this hotel behind Saint-Sulpice. It came on to rain and I had to run from the Métro station and got there in a muck sweat.' This wasn't bad – I'd been expecting a brilliant spring day with accordionists serenading him through the Jardins du Luxembourg. 'I got to the room, Chappie was there, took off my hat and coat. Wasn't planning to get starkers in front of mine host, as you might imagine. He said, "Don't worry, she'll do the rest." He just sat me down on the bed, wrapped this scarf around my head, knotted it twice, made me promise as an Englishman not to do any peeping, and left the room. A couple of minutes later I heard the door open.'

My uncle put down his whisky, set his head back and closed his eyes, closing them to remember something he had not in any case seen. Indulgently, I let him drag out the pause. At last he said, 'And then the next day. Again. Raining again too.'

The gas-fire noisily held its breath, the ice-cubes trilled promptingly in my glass. But Uncle Freddy didn't seem to want to continue. Or perhaps he'd really stopped. That wouldn't do. It was – how shall I put it? – like narrative cock-teasing.

'So?'

'So,' my uncle repeated softly. 'Just so.'

We sat quietly for a minute or two until I couldn't avoid the question. 'And what *was* the difference?'

Uncle Freddy, head back and eyes still squeezed together, uttered a noise between a sigh and a whimper. Eventually he said, 'The French lass licked the raindrops from my face.' He opened his eyes again, and showed me his tears.

I was strangely moved. I was also wearily suspicious, but this didn't stop me being moved. *The French lass licked the raindrops from my face.* I gave my uncle – whether plausible liar or sentimental remembrancer – the gift of my envy.

'You could tell?'

'Tell what?' He seemed half absent, being tweaked and tickled by memories.

'Which one was English and which one was French?'

'Oh yes, I could tell.'

'How?'

'How do you think?'

'Smell of garlic?'

He chuckled. 'No. They both wore scent as a matter of fact. Quite strong scent. Not the same, of course.'

'So . . . they did different things? Or was it the way they did it?'

'Trade secret.' Now he was beginning to look smug again.

'Come off it, Uncle Freddy.'

'Always made it a rule never to snitch on my lady friends.'

'Uncle Freddy, you never set eyes on them. They were provided for you. They weren't your lady friends.'

'They were to me. Both of them. That's what they felt like. That's what I've always considered them.'

This was exasperating, not least because I'd been drawn into giving credence to my uncle's fantasy. And what was the point of inventing a story and then withdrawing the key facts?

'But you can tell me, Uncle, because you told them.'

'Them?'

'The group. You reported to them the next day.'

'Well, an Englishman's word is his bond except when it isn't. You've lived long enough to know that. And besides . . . the truth is I had a feeling, not so much the first time but more strongly the second, that I was being watched.'

'Someone in the wardrobe?'

'I don't know. How, where. Just sensed it, somehow. It made me feel a bit grubby. And as I say, I made it a rule never to snitch on my lady friends. So I took the boat-train home the next day.'

Forgetting about the motor-rally, or the career in authentic wax polish, or whatever else it might have been.

'And *that*', my uncle continued, 'was the cleverest thing I ever did.' He looked at me as if his whole story had been aimed at this moment. 'Because that's where I met your Aunt Kate. On the boat-train.'

'I never knew that.'

'No reason why you should. Engaged within the month, married within three.'

A busy spring indeed. 'And what did *she* think of your adventure?'

His face shut down again. 'Your Aunt Kate was as pure as driven snow. I'd no more have talked about that than . . . pick my teeth in public.'

'You never told her?'

'Never breathed a word. Anyway, imagine it from her side. She meets this likely fellow, gets a bit soft on him, asks what he's been up to in Paris, and he tells her he's been knocking off lasses at the rate of one a day after promising to go back afterwards and talk smut about them. She'd not be soft on him for long, would she?'

In my limited observation, Aunt Kate and Uncle Freddy had been a devoted couple. His grief at her death, even when exaggerated into melodrama by drink, had seemed quite genuine. The fact that he survived her by six years I attributed to no more than the enforced habit of living. Two months after this final birthday evening, he gave up that habit. The funeral was the usual sparse and awkward business: a Surrealist wreath with an obscene motif might have helped.

Five years later the *Recherches sur la sexualité* appeared, and my uncle's story was partly corroborated. My curiosity and frustration were also revived; I was left staring at the same old questions. I resented the fact that my uncle had clammed up, leaving me with nothing but *The French lass licked the raindrops from my face.*

As I have mentioned, my uncle's encounter with the Surrealist Group was relegated to a mere appendix. The *Recherches* are of course extensively annotated: preface, introduction, text, appendices, footnotes to text, footnotes to appendices, footnotes to footnotes. Probably I am the only person to have spotted something which is at most only of family interest. Footnote 23 to Session 5(a) states that the Englishman referred to as 'T.F.' was on one occasion the subject of what is described as an 'attempted vindication of Surrealist theory (cf. note 12 to Appendix 3)', but that no record of the results obtained has survived. Footnote 12 to Appendix 3 describes these 'attempted vindications' and mentions that in a few of them there was an Englishwoman involved. This woman is referred to simply as 'K'.

I have only two final reflections on the matter. The first

is that when scientists employ volunteers to help with their research projects, they often withhold from these participants the true purpose of the test, for fear such knowledge might, wittingly or unwittingly, affect the purity of the process and the accuracy of the result.

The second thought came to me only quite recently. I may have mentioned that I take a novice interest in wine. I belong to a small group which meets twice a month: we each take along a bottle and the wines are tasted blind. Usually we get them wrong, sometimes we get them right, though what is wrong and what is right in this matter is a complicated business. If a wine tastes to you like a young Australian Chardonnay, then that in a sense is what it is. The label may subsequently declare it to be an expensive burgundy, but if it hasn't been that in your mouth, then that is what it can never truly become.

This isn't quite what I meant to say. I meant to say that a couple of weeks ago we had a guest tutor. She was a well-known Master of Wine, and she told us an interesting fact. Apparently if you take a magnum and decant it into two separate bottles and put them into a blind tasting, then it's extremely rare for even wily drinkers to guess that the wine in those two particular bottles is in fact the same one. People expect all the wines to be different, and their palates therefore insist that they are. She said it was a most revealing experiment, and that it almost always works.

# MELON

My dearest cousin—

A week before Mr Hawkins & I departed, you rallied me with pretty mockery concerning the vanity of my expedition—that the company I should seek out would be that which most resembled my own, & the resultant experiences no more than the mutual licking of bear cubs—& you told me that I should come home refined & polished like a Dutch skipper from a whale-fishing. It is for this reason that I lately ordered changes to our itinerary—& if I should die from the attack of brigands, the negligence of a rural physician, or the venom of a viper, you shall be the cause, Mademoiselle Evelina—since it was your doing that we left our course for Italy and have come to Montpelier. Mr Hawkins proffered some remarks upon our altered destination—that he would never have known you such an authority on the French geography having not ventured closer to Gaul than the library at Nesfield.

My observations about brigands & vipers were not of a serious nature, Evelina—you are not to imagine that they are, or that you would be responsible were anything to befal Mr Hawkins & myself—besides he is armed with a musquetoon as I have told you which must discourage both brigands & vipers. Montpelier is in any case a handsome

city—it is bien percée to use the French expression, &
indeed such a Galloman have I become that I scarcely
remember the English equivalences of the French
expressions I employ. It is, as we would express the matter,
a finely laid out city—we are lodged at the Cheval Blanc
which is accounted the finest auberge in the town, yet Mr
Hawkins condemns it for a squalid hovel where the traveller
is plucked like a bird of passage, with every hand reaching
out to pull a feather. Mr Hawkins has a low view of the
French hostelries, which he maintains have not improved in
quality since last he was in France at the time of Charlemagne
while you were still in the nursery, dear cousin—but I
have a more generous or tolerant disposition in the
matter—& besides all this, it is anyway part of Hawkins'
employment to argue prices & deal with knaves. You did not
demand letters from me in order to be told this, I am certain.
Montpelier is a handsome city & a place of pilgrimage to
those in ill health which will no doubt please Mama—the
butter is peculiar but in my view rather fine, being pure
white and resembling hair pomade in appearance—we
could not find hot water to make our tea in several
consecutive establishments, which displeased my scowling
tutor as you will imagine, & he did not respond to my
suggestion that the heat of the day did service for the
missing heat of the water. He is inclined to behave toward
me as if he were a physician & I some feeble-minded boy,
which I find most vexing. He claims to find my renewed
cheerfulness excessive for the circumstances, as I do his
impertinence. On our route to Montpelier not far short eight
leagues or so we passed through Nismes and were able to
view the Roman antiquities on whose subject Mr Hawkins

had a good deal to say—the Pont Du Garde is indeed a worthy edifice which I have sketched for your pleasure.

After Lyons we travelled through Burgundy which afforded us the instruction of observing the vandange. The very hills and mountains of this region seem laid out by God so that the vines which cover every slope from the northern to southern extremity receive the fullest generosity of Phaeton. The bunches of grapes lie like pearls on the branches & even entwined with the thorns & thickets of the hedgerow—Mr Hawkins & I felt enjoined to essay the consequence of their crushing—in truth the burgundy wine we found there was watery & lacking in strength compared to any one might purchase in London & my fancy for obtaining a hogshead of the new vintage on our return was discarded by the road's side—it is probable therefore that the best wine of burgundy is exported & sold abroad—for when we reached the Dauphiné we drank wine called ermitage which contained such strength we could not find in burgundy—it sold for three livres the bottle—we also discovered an iron-wheeled engine known as an <u>alembic</u> which trundles from village to village for the purpose of distilling the local wine into liquor—this will not be of the greatest interest to you, I fear.

I blush at the memory of my first letters—& would have them back if there were a manner for effecting this— they were the letters of a young cub, & a spoiled one who missed his cousin & judged difference mere peculiarity— yet I still believe that the stinking macquerel & the sallad made of stinking oil & the omelet made of stinking eggs that we were obliged by hunger to devour in Saint Omer were all truthfully described. But I had not then shrugged off my melancholy and I regret that on occasions suspicion and hostility overcame me. That the postilions wear pigtail queues and vault into boots the size of milkchurns while still encumbered by their shoes—that the gentlemen of Paris carry umbrellas over the heads on fine days against the sun—that the same gentlemen employ the service of barbers for their dogs—that the horses are ratty in aspect—that lemonade is sold in the streets—I have come to a warmer understanding of such things than I had at the time—& a warmer understanding than the frequently perspiring & foul-tempered Mr Hawkins will perhaps ever do.

It is true however that some of the inns are indeed squalid & that we have more than once witnessed—no, my dear, you do not need to be informed of such things, especially in a letter which your sister might take from your grasp. There are two aspects to this country which Frenchified as I am I yet accustom myself to with much difficulty—the infernal division of the calendar into jours maigres & jours gras—we incessantly hear the cry of jour maigre whenever the stomach craves a good beefsteak— the French would rather commit foul murder than devour the wrong part of God's creation on the wrong day—it is all most vexing & God bless England for the land of reason. Nor can I accustom myself to the lack of a pretty girl to gaze upon—in truth they are a swarthy race & from Boulogne to Paris & from Paris to Lyons we saw naught but women who might as well be muleteers—in a hostelry southward of Lyons as we were about our dinner at last a pretty girl entered & the whole company French & travellers gave her the tribute of applause to which she was evidently accustomed—you must not mind any of this—I cast my eyes upon the locket each night before I say my prayers.

The common people are much dirtier than the common
people in England—they are meagre & half-starved—
yet their starvation is not such as to prevent them from ill
humour, indecency & crime—they are an impulsive race
of course—in Montpelier I witnessed a coachman whip a
horse which had fallen to its knees on the street & could
not get up—it was a savage sight—Hawkins forbade me
to intervene as I would have done at Nesfield—& when
he was through whipping the beast his master emerged from
the house & gave the coachman a whipping in his turn
until the fellow was on his knees like the horse beside
him—then the master retired into the house & the
coachman flung his arms around the neck of the horse—I
draw no lesson from this but if I were to begin the narrative
of the cruelties I have seen you would enjoin me to return
without ever setting my eyes upon Italy.

The people of quality are in my judgment more
attentive to their own persons than in England—while
our common people are less dirty & less slovenly than their
French equivalences—the people of quality here would
not neglect their external dress as the English might happily
do—the Frenchman must have his laced coat & powdered
hair & must appear clean & well-dressed—nevertheless his
house will often be filled with litter & dirt such as an
Englishman would not abide—it is almost a riddle from
the nursery would you have an orderly man in a disorderly
house or a disorderly man in an orderly house?—ask that
of your tutor when next he entertains you with moral
philosophy. We have witnessed the filth & disarray of their
houses because of their natural hospitality & warmth which they
extend even to a bear cub and his ill-humoured tutor—
they are indeed the friendliest & most welcoming race I

have met although you will say that my evidence is less than it could be but I have been in Edinburgh do not forget.

I have enquired most particularly of many persons of quality concerning the sports they practise and have received little information—there is racing of course—there is hunting—there is gaming which subject I have not mentioned to you in this letter, dear cousin—the common people have their separate entertainments as you may expect—I cannot however find that there is sport such as is practised in England—this is a weakness in a nation as I believe. This is all dull for you.

Last night we were served small birds called grives which not having the dictionary about us we were unable to identify—they were presented wrapped in vine leaves & were roasted but still the blood ran from them when cut— Mr Hawkins could not abide this as being raw meat—it was explained that if the roasting is protracted the juice is lost—you must run to the dictionary and discover what manner of creature we ate—there are also red partridges twice the size of our British ones—you will now be as sleepy reading as I am writing—goodnight my cousin.

<u>Post scriptum</u>. Mr Hawkins surmises that I might have neglected to inform you of all the intricacies of all the antiquities of Nismes & of the Pont Du Garde—how many tiers how many arches how many feet of height what order of architecture does it belong to? Tuscan Mr Hawkins—it is like being still in the schoolroom—whether or not the ancients did exceed us in beauty as we exceed them in convenience—Evelina, you exceed all the ancients in beauty—I have assured Mr Hawkins that you have been informed of all the matter he poured into my ears while I was sketching—I would count upon him to catechise you

on our return—I am so fond of you my dear & you do
miss me a little I trust—my melancholy is quite
dispersed—I swore at myself for a fool on our coming to
Montpelier for I cannot expect a letter from you until we
reach Nice or even Genoa.

There is a great amount of religion in this country—
priests and monks abound—we have seen many churches
adorned with many statues in niches on their front end—
Mr Hawkins will know the name for it—I have temporarily
forgot—we do not enter many of them except for curiosity
as to the antiquities—there is much silver & much
coloured glass & the incense takes the nostrils like snuff so
that my handkerchief is a constant requirement—there
are large crucifixes at the cross roads & within the fields—
there are many protestants in this city & they are well and
kindly governed—however according to the laws of France
a protestant minister may not perform his acts of
worship—one such was hanged in the market place for
doing so.

You cannot imagine the melons we have been devouring
since we reached the southern extremity of the country—
from the esplanade where we walk there is a prospect of the
Mediterranean Sea to one quarter & the Sevennes
Mountains to the opposite one—you would not think that
the fruit so prized & pampered at Nesfield—so protected
from the red spider—could be so easy & abundant in
another place—it is like another species the flesh rich &
golden & sweet & fragrant—it would turn me voluptuary
or at least Frenchman—even Mr Hawkins by the
testimony of reliable witnesses has been seen to smile as it
is deposited before him. As you see, my mother's
apprehensions as to my disposition are quite misplaced.

My dear Evelina, your cousin is not greatly improved as a letter-writer by his travels—the truth is I suffer an awkwardness with the pen which I rarely feel when I am before you—so you shall continue to mock me for a Dutch whale fisher—present my honourable respects to your Father and Mother—I dream of your delicate hand awaiting me at Nice.

Your loving cousin
Hamilton Lindsay

———————— ○ ————————

Sir Hamilton Lindsay departed for Chertsey on Thursday, 6th August. Samuel Dobson travelled on top with the groom, Sir Hamilton inside with the cricket bats. This was, he knew without reflection, the correct priority: Dobson would only be toughened by rain and rough weather, whereas the bats were more sensitive to the displeasure of the elements and must be treated with care. In tedious moments of the journey, Sir Hamilton would take out a soft cloth and gently rub a little butter into the blade of his bat. Others preferred oil, but he felt a certain local pride in this particularity of his. The instrument itself was carved from a branch of willow hewn on his own estate; now it was being swabbed with butter made from the milk of cows which had grazed in the very water-meadow at whose edge the willows grew.

He finished soothing his bat and wound around it the yard of muslin within which it always travelled. Dobson's bat was a cruder engine, and Dobson no doubt had his own secrets for making it as strong and supple as he required. Some men rubbed ale into their bats; others the fat of a ham; others again were said to warm their bats before the fire and then make water upon them. No doubt the moon had to be in a certain quarter at the same time, thought Sir Hamilton with a sceptical jerk of the head. The only thing that counted was how you smote the ball; and Dobson could smite with the best of them. But it was the persistency and valour of the man's right arm that had persuaded Sir Hamilton to bring him to Nesfield.

Dobson was the second under-gardener at the Hall. It was not, however, to Dobson that a man would readily turn for the implementation of a landscape by the late Mr Brown. The fellow could scarce tell a lupin from a turnip, and his duties were confined to the physical and the general rather than to the skilled and the particular. In short, he was not permitted to handle a spade without the presence of an overseer. But Sir Hamilton had not offered him employment – or played the poacher, to use the description of Dobson's previous employer – with the intention of procuring a lady-fingered turf-trimmer. Dobson's expertise was with another kind of turf. To witness the man's unflinchingness when standing at bat's end was sure compensation for his failure of wit in the kitchen garden.

They would arrive at Chertsey the next day, and then proceed for Dover on the Saturday. Five of the Duke's cricketers lived hard by Chertsey: Fry, Edmeads, Attfield, Etheridge and Wood. Then there was to be himself, Dobson, the Earl of Tankerville, William Bedster and Lumpy Stevens. The Duke was naturally in Paris; Tankerville and Bedster were coming separately to Dover; so eight of them would meet at Mr Yalden's inn at Chertsey. It was here, some years back, that Lumpy Stevens had won Tankerville his famous bet. The Earl had wagered that his man could in practice-bowling hit a feather placed on the ground one time in four.

Mr Stevens had obliged his employer, who, it was rumoured, had profited by several hundred pounds in the business. Lumpy Stevens was one of Tankerville's gardeners, and Sir Hamilton had often set himself musing over the prospect of a separate wager with the Earl: as to which of their two men knew the less about horticulture.

He admitted to a gloomy and irritable mood as he ignored the passing countryside. Mr Hawkins had declined the invitation to accompany him on the journey. Hamilton had urged his former tutor to cast his eyes upon the Continent of Europe one last time. More than that, he thought it a damned generous offer on his behalf to cart the old fellow across to Paris and back, no doubt enduring many gross and whining episodes of vomit on the packet, if the past were any indicator of the present. But Mr Hawkins had answered that he preferred his memories of tranquillity to a vision of the present troubles. He saw no prospect of excitement in the matter, grateful as he was to Sir Hamilton. Grateful and pusillanimous, Sir Hamilton reflected as he took his leave of the broken-kneed old man. As pusillanimous as Evelina, who had poured thunderstorms from her eyes in an attempt to thwart his departure. Twice he had discovered her in hugger-mugger with Dobson, and had been unable to obtain from either the matter of their discussions. Dobson claimed that he was trying to lighten Milady's burden of apprehension and fear regarding the voyage, but Sir Hamilton did not entirely believe him. What did they have to fear anyway? The two nations were not at war, their mission was peaceful, and no Frenchman, however untutored, would ever mistake Sir Hamilton for one of his own race. And besides, there would be eleven of them, all stout fellows armed with pieces of English willow. What possible harm could befall them?

At Chertsey they put up at The Cricketers, where Mr Yalden gave them good hospitality and regretted that his cricketing days were now in the past. Others regretted this less than Mr Yalden, since their host had not always shown himself scrupulous when the laws of the game impeded him from winning. He was, however, scrupulous in launching his Chertsey men and their compatriots off to war with his strongest hogshead. Hamilton lay in bed with an image of the beefsteak in his stomach tossing on a sea of ale like the Dover packet in a Channel storm.

His emotions were scarcely less turbulent. Evelina's water-spouts had affected him the more because she had never, in their ten years of marriage, sought to deter him from any of his cricketing ventures. She was not like Jack Heythrop's wife, or Sir James Tinker's: ladies who shrank from the notion of their husbands consorting on the turf with blacksmiths and gamekeepers, chimney-sweeps and shoeboys. Mrs Jack Heythrop, her nose pointing to Heaven, would ask how you might expect to exert your authority over the coachman and the gardener when the previous afternoon the coachman had caught you out and the gardener had shown such disrespect to your bowling? It did not make for social harmony, and the sporting universe should be a reflection of the social universe. Hence, according to Mrs Heythrop, the manifest superiority and virtue of racing: owner, trainer, jockey and groom all knew their places, and such places were of themselves fixed by their self-evident importance. How different from the foolish commingling of cricket, which was besides, as everyone knew, little more than a vulgar excuse for gambling.

Of course there was gambling. What was the point of sport if a man did not gamble? What was the point of a glass of soda if it did not have brandy in it? Wagering, as Tanker-ville had once put it, was the salt which brought out the savour of the dish. Nowadays Hamilton himself wagered modestly, just as he had promised Evelina and his mother before his marriage. In his present mood, however, and having regard to the money he had saved by Mr Hawkins' absence, he was damned inclined to wager a little above the normal on the outcome of the match between Dorset's XI and the Gentlemen of France. To be sure, some of the Chertsey fellows were becoming a little dull of eye and plump of shank. But if Dorset's men could not have the beating of Monsieur, then they should turn their bats into winter kindling.

They left Chertsey by post-coach on the morning of Sunday, 9th August. Approaching Dover, they encountered several carriages of French making towards London.

'Running away from the bowling of Mr Stevens, I shouldn't doubt,' observed Sir Hamilton.

'Best not to bowl full tilt, Lumpy,' said Dobson, 'or they'll be filling their breeches.'

'So will you, Dobson, if you dine French-style too often,' replied Stevens.

Sir Hamilton had a sudden memory, and recited to the occupants of the post-coach the lines:

> She sent her priest in wooden shoes
> From haughty Gaul to make ragoos.

Inchoate murmurings greeted the verse, and Sir Hamilton caught Dobson's eyes upon him, their expression more that of an anxious tutor than of a second under-gardener.

At Dover they met the Earl of Tankerville and William Bedster at an inn already over-crowded with emigrant

French. Bedster had formerly been the Earl's butler and the most celebrated bat in Surrey; now he was a publican in Chelsea, and his retirement had helped increase his circumference. He and the Chertsey men taunted one another over their last English dinner with the contentious happenings of forgotten seasons, and noisily argued the merits of two-stump cricket over its modern replacement. In another corner of the inn sat Tankerville and Sir Hamilton Lindsay, ruminating upon the general situation in France and the particular position of their friend John Sackville, third Duke of Dorset and His Majesty's Ambassador, these six years past, to the Court of Versailles. Such matters were not for the ears of Lumpy Stevens and the Chertsey men.

Dorset's embassy had from the beginning been conducted in a manner to make Mrs Jack Heythrop tip her nose in disapproval. His hospitality in Paris was of the most generous kind, embracing under its roof gamesters and card-sharps, wh---s and parasites. His intimacy with many of the finest ladies of French society extended, it was said, even as far as Mrs Bourbon herself. It was whispered — yet especially not before the likes of either Mrs Jack Heythrop or Mr Lumpy Stevens — that Dorset even lived *en famille* at Versailles. The mundane business of mere diplomacy he left to his friend Mr Hailes.

Ever since his appointment in 1783, the Duke had thought nothing of returning to England annually for the cricketing months. But this summer he had failed to appear. From such absence, rather than from the ubiquitous presence of French refugees in London, Tankerville and Lindsay had judged the current disturbances across the Channel to be of proper gravity. As the summer had proceeded and public order deteriorated in the French capital, scoundrels began

issuing libels on the British nation, and rumours were started
of the Royal Navy blockading French ports. In these darken-
ing circumstances Dorset had proposed, towards the end of
July, as a gesture of conciliation and friendship between the
two countries, that a team of English cricketers be sent to
play a team of Frenchmen in the Champs-Elysées. The Duke,
who during his six years had done much to foment interest
in the game, was to organise the eleven Parisians; Tankerville
was enjoined to arrange transport of the English players with
all despatch.

Sir Hamilton lay in bed that night recalling his tour with
Mr Hawkins a dozen, no, nearer fifteen years ago. He himself
was now becoming almost as plump of shank as many of
the Chertsey fellows. He remembered the ratty horses and the
lank pigtail queues trailing down like an eel; the stinking
macquerel and the voluptuous melon; the coachman and his
horse, kneeling in whipped equality; the blood running from
the roast thrushes when the knife was inserted. He imagined
himself smiting the French bowling to all parts of the
Champs-Elysées, and Frenchmen carrying barbered dogs
applauding him from beneath their umbrellas. He imagined
seeing the French coast approach; he remembered being
happy.

Sir Hamilton Lindsay was never put to the test on the
Elysian Fields, nor did Lumpy Stevens ever make Frenchmen
fill their breeches as they received his demon bowling.
Instead, Lumpy Stevens played at Bishopsbourne in the match
between Kent and Surrey, watched by several Chertsey men
and Sir Hamilton Lindsay. Their *rendez-vous* with Dorset had
not taken place, as originally intended, at the Duke's *hôtel* in
Paris, but on the quayside of Dover in the morning of
Monday, 10th August 1789. The Duke had relinquished his

embassy two days previously, and had travelled the 90 miles to Boulogne on roads even more infested with bandits than was usual. It was presumed that Dorset's *hôtel* had been plundered by the mob within hours of his departure; but in spite of this he was in remarkably cheerful spirits. He was, he said, much looking forward to spending the late summer and autumn in England as he normally did. The French capital would not seem so far away, since many of his Parisian friends had now come to England. He would discover whether there were enough among their number for the match which had been intended for the Champs-Elysées to be played instead at Sevenoaks.

———————— o ————————

General Sir Hamilton Lindsay and his wife walked to the church every Sunday afternoon. It was in truth a strange pilgrimage, since he would as soon step inside a mosque or a synagogue as inside a papistical shrine. Yet the fact that the church had been reduced and was now quite inactive drew much poison from the visit. Besides, it was the kind of ambulation he required if appetite for his dinner was to be provoked. Lady Lindsay had insisted on such bestirring of the shanks ever since she had been permitted out to join him.

A lieutenant would accompany them at a discreet distance, which did not offend Sir Hamilton, even though he had given his word in the matter as a soldier and a gentleman. The French maintained that the officer was present in case the General and his wife needed protection from some of the coarser local patriots; and he was prepared to connive in this diplomatic mendacity. No doubt General de Rauzan was receiving the same courteous caretaking at his villa near Roehampton.

Elements of the revolutionary army had passed through the village on their march to Lyon a dozen or so years earlier. The bells of the church had been taken down; the silver and copper removed; the priest encouraged either to marry or to flee. Three cannoneers had set up their engine opposite the west door and had used the saints in their niches for target practice. As the General observed each week – an observation which always put him into a brief good humour – their accuracy had evidently been as nothing compared with that of Lumpy Stevens. Books had been incinerated, doors taken from their hinges; colour had been bludgeoned from the stained-glass. The soldiers had even begun demolition of the south wall, and upon departing had left instruction that the church was to be used as a quarry. The villagers, however, had shown pious obstinacy, and not a stone had been removed; even so, wind and diagonal rain swept uncivilly through the injured edifice.

On their return, dinner would be laid out beneath the awning on the terrace, and Dobson would be standing awk-wardly behind Lady Lindsay's chair. In the General's view, the fellow had managed his successive translations with some skill: cricketer, gardener, infantryman, and now major-domo, manservant and chief forager. The very suddenness of their impromptu *ménage* had naturally given licence for a little more informality than would have been permitted at Nesfield; even so, the General was surprised that while addressing his beloved Evelina, his glance would increasingly slide up beyond her bonnet to Dobson standing behind her. At times he damned well found himself addressing Dobson, as if expecting him to join in the conversation. Happily the fellow was sufficiently trained never to catch his master's eye on such occasions, and besides knew how to feign a proper deafness. Evelina, for her part, treated her husband's divergence from social form as if it were mere eccentricity, to be accounted for by his long exile and lack of intercourse. He was indeed much changed when she had come out three years ago: he had grown corpulent – no doubt from the unfavourable diet – but also indolent and weary. She had not doubted his pleasure at seeing her again; but found that his mind now travelled only in the past. It was natural that he should think so hard upon England, but England should also represent the future. That was what she enjoined him to hope: one day, they would surely return. There had been dismaying rumours that Buonaparte felt little zeal for the return of General de Rauzan to the ranks of his higher command; and it was true that the Frenchman's notorious docility in permitting himself to be captured by Sir John Stuart at Maida could well displease any commander. But such rumours must be dismissed, she believed; hope must be made to flicker. England, England and the future, she urged upon him. But in the General's mind England seemed to represent only the past, and he was connected to that past as much by Dobson as by his wife.

'Those cannoneers, my dear. Had they but half the skill of Lumpy Stevens, they should have not wasted so much shot.'

'That is quite true, Hamilton.'

Lumpy could hit a feather placed upon the ground one time out of four in practice bowling. More than one time out of four. He had won the bet for Tankerville at Chertsey. Lumpy had been the Earl's gardener. How many of them now were buried in the soil?

'Dorset was never again the same man,' he continued, easing the remnants of his cutlet to the side of his plate. 'He retired to Knole and received nobody.' Sir Hamilton had it on authority that the Duke had kept to his room like an anchorite, and that his only pleasure was to hear the music of muted violins playing from the other side of his door.

'I had heard that the family was disposed to melancholy.'

'Dorset was always the liveliest fellow,' the General replied. 'Before.' This was true; and at first he had remained so after his return from France. That autumn there had been cricketing as there had been all their lives. But as Knole filled with *émigrés* the situation in France had brought dark clouds to Dorset's mind. There had been letters exchanged with Mrs Bourbon, and many considered the loss of that intimacy to be the immediate cause of his melancholia. It was repeated, not always in the warmest of spirits, that upon quitting Paris the Duke had made a gift of his cricket bat to Mrs Bourbon, and that the lady had preserved this attribute of British manliness in her closet, just as Dido had hung up the galligaskins of the departed Aeneas. The General did not know the particularities of this rumour. He knew only that Dorset had continued cricketing at Sevenoaks until the season's end of 1791 – the very same summer in which Mrs Bourbon and her husband had undertaken their flight to Varennes. They had been recaptured, and Dorset had cricketed no more. This was all the General could say, except that Dorset, thinning the noise of the world to muted violins heard through a wooden door, had not lived to learn the murderous news of the 16th October 1793.

God knew he was no Papist, but the cannoneers and fusiliers of the revolutionary army were no Protestant gentlemen either. They had taken the crucifixes from the fields and made an *auto-da-fé* of them. They had paraded asses and mules wearing the vestments of bishops. They had burnt prayer books and manuals of instruction. They had forced priests into marriage and ordered French men and French women to spit upon the image of Christ. They had taken their knives to altarpieces and their hammers to the heads of saints. They had dismantled the bells and taken them to foundries where they were cast into cannon with which to bombard fresh churches. They had expunged Christianity from the land, and what had been their reward? Buonaparte.

Buonaparte, war, famine, false dreams of conquest and the contempt of Europe. It grieved the General that this should be the case. He had many times been rallied by his fellow officers for being a Galloman. It was a fact he would acknowledge, and in honest justification would adduce evidence as to the national character such as he had observed it. But he also knew that the true source of his inclination lay much in the effects of memory. He judged it probable that all gentlemen of his age in some way loved themselves when young, and naturally extended such tenderness to the surrounding circumstances of their youth. For Sir Hamilton, this time had been that of his tour with Mr Hawkins. Now he had returned to France, but it was to a country changed and reduced. He had lost his youth: well, every living soul lost that. But he had also lost his England and his France. Did they expect him to endure that also? His mind had become a little more steady since they had permitted Evelina and Dobson to join him. Yet there were times when he knew what that poor devil Dorset felt, except that for him there was no door and the violins were not muted.

'Dorset, Tankerville, Stevens, Bedster, myself, Dobson, Attfield, Fry, Etheridge, Edmeads . . .'

'The lieutenant has procured for us a melon, my dear.'

'Whom do I forget? Whom do I damned forget? Why is it always the same one?' The General stared across at his wife, who was poised to carve – what? A cricket ball? A cannonball? The violins were scrabbling at his ears like insects. 'Whom do I forget?' He leaned forwards on his elbows, and covered his eyelids with his fattened finger-ends. Dobson quickly bent his head towards Lady Lindsay.

'You forget Mr Wood, I believe, my dear,' she murmured.

'*Wood.*' The General took his fingers from his eyes, smiled at his wife, and nodded as Dobson lowered a slice of orange melon before him. 'Wood. He was not a Chertsey man?'

Lady Lindsay was unable to seek assistance with this enquiry, since her husband's eyes were upon her. So she answered cautiously, 'I have not heard so.'

'No, Wood was never a Chertsey man. You are right, my dear. Let us forget him.' The General dusted sugar on his melon. 'He had never been in France, of course. Dorset, Tankerville, myself, that is all. Dobson, of course, has been in France subsequently. I wonder what they would have made of Lumpy Stevens?'

Lumpy Stevens had won Tankerville's bet for him. Lumpy Stevens could hit a feather one time in four at practice-bowling. The French cannoneers . . .

'Perhaps we may expect a letter tomorrow, my dear.'

'A letter? From Mr Wood? I very much doubt that. Mr Wood is almost certainly cricketing with the Angel Gabriel at this very minute on the turf of the Elysian Fields. He must be dead and buried by now. They all must. Though Dobson is not, of course. No, Dobson is not.' The General glanced up above his wife's bonnet. Dobson was there, staring straight ahead, unhearing.

Dorset's embassy in Paris had prospered. There had been complaints against him of the usual kind. Nowadays the world was ruled by Mrs Jack Heythrop and her sisters. But *The Times* had reported in 1787 that as a consequence of the Duke's presence and example, racing in France had begun to decline, and the pursuit of cricket had begun to take its place, as making better use of the French turf. It had surprised the General that the young lieutenant who spied on them had been unaware of this, until, the calculation being done, it was shown that the fellow would scarcely have said farewell to his wet-nurse at the time.

The mob had burnt Dorset's *hôtel* in Paris. They had burnt prayer books and manuals of instruction. What had become of Dorset's cricket bat? Had they burnt that too? We were about to embark at Dover on the morning of the 10th when whom should we see but the Duke. On the quay, the mail packet at anchor behind him. In good spirits, too. Therefore we had gone to Bishopsbourne to dine with Sir Horace Mann, and the following day the match between Kent and Surrey . . .

'Dorset, Tankerville, Stevens, Bedster, myself . . .'

'The melon is sweet, do you not find?'

'Dobson, Attfield, Fry, Etheridge, Edmeads . . .'

'I think tomorrow we shall expect a letter.'

'Whom do I forget? Whom do I forget?'

The physician, though French, had seemed a reasonable man to Lady Lindsay. He was a student and follower of Pinel. The melancholia in his view must not be permitted to develop into *démence*. The General must be offered diversions. He must go for walks as often as he could be persuaded. He was to be allowed no more than one glass of wine with his dinner. He must be reminded of pleasant moments from the past. It had been the physician's opinion that, despite the evident improvement in the General's condition brought about by the presence of Madame, it might be advisable to send for the man Dobson, to whom the General made such frequent allusion that the doctor had at first taken him to be the patient's son. It would be necessary, of course, to place a guard upon Sir Hamilton, but it would be as discreet as possible. It was regrettable that, according to the physician's private information, there was no immediate prospect of the proposed exchange being effected, and of the Englishman returning to his own country. Unfortunately, it appeared that the family and advocates of General de Rauzan had repeatedly failed to persuade those close to the Emperor of the Frenchman's military importance.

'Whom do I forget?'

'You forget Mr Wood.'

'Mr Wood, I knew it. He was a Chertsey man, was he not?'

'I am almost sure of it.'

'He was, he was indeed a Chertsey man. A fine fellow, Wood.'

Normally he remembered Wood. It was Etheridge whom he forgot. Etheridge or Edmeads. Once he had forgotten himself. He had the other ten names but could not seize the eleventh. How could this happen, that a man forgets himself?

The General had risen to his feet, an empty wine glass in his hand. 'My dear,' he began, addressing his wife but looking at Dobson, 'when I reflect upon the terrible history of this country, which I myself first visited in the year of Our Lord 1774 . . .'

'The melon,' said his wife lightly.

'. . . and which, since that time, has suffered so much

travail. There is a certain conclusion which I should like to venture . . .'

No, it must be averted. It was never beneficial. At first she had smiled at the reflection, but it led to melancholia, always to melancholia.

'Do you require more of this melon, Hamilton?' she asked in a forceful voice.

'It appears to me that the terrible events of that terrible year, of all those terrible years, which placed our two countries so far apart from one another, which led to this terrible war, such events might have been avoided, indeed could have been avoided by something which on first examination you might judge a mere fancy . . .'

'Hamilton!' The wife had risen in her turn, but the husband still gazed beyond her at the impassive Dobson. '*Hamilton!*' When he continued not to hear her, she took her wine glass and cast it on to the terrace.

The screeching violins ceased. The General returned her gaze, and shyly sat down again. 'Oh well, my dear,' he said, 'it was only an idle notion of mine. The melon is ripe, is it not? Shall we each have another slice?'

# EVERMORE

---------------------------------  ○  ---------------------------------

ALL THE TIME she carried them with her, in a bag
knotted at the neck. She had bayoneted the polythene
with a fork, so that condensation would not gather and
begin to rot the frail card. She knew what happened when you
covered seedlings in a flower-pot: damp came from nowhere to
make its sudden climate. This had to be avoided. There had
been so much wet back then, so much rain, churned mud
and drowned horses. She did not mind it for herself. She
minded it for them still, for all of them, back then.

There were three postcards, the last he had sent. The
earlier ones had been divided up, lost perhaps, but she had
the last of them, his final evidence. On the day itself, she
would unknot the bag and trace her eyes over the jerky
pencilled address, the formal signature (initials and surname
only), the obedient crossings-out. For many years she had
ached at what the cards did not say; but nowadays she found
something in their official impassivity which seemed proper,
even if not consoling.

Of course she did not need actually to look at them, any
more than she needed the photograph to recall his dark eyes,
sticky-out ears, and the jaunty smile which agreed that the
fun would be all over by Christmas. At any moment she could
bring the three pieces of buff field-service card exactly to

mind. The dates: Dec 24, Jan 11, Jan 17, written in his own hand, and confirmed by the postmark which added the years: 16, 17, 17. 'NOTHING is to be written on this side except the date and signature of the sender. Sentences not required may be erased. <u>If anything else is added the postcard will be destroyed.</u>' And then the brutal choices.

```
I am quite well
I have been admitted into hospital
      ⎰sick   ⎱   and am going on well
      ⎱wounded⎰   and hope to be discharged soon
I am being sent down to the base
                        ⎰letter dated .......
I have received your  ⎰telegram..........
                        ⎱parcel............
Letter follows at first opportunity
I have received no letter from you
      ⎰Lately
      ⎱For a long time
```

He was quite well on each occasion. He had never been admitted into hospital. He was not being sent down to the base. He had received a letter of a certain date. A letter would follow at the first opportunity. He had not received no letter. All done with thick pencilled crossing-out and a single date. Then, beside the instruction <u>Signature only</u>, the last signal from her brother. S. Moss. A large looping S with a circling full stop after it. Then Moss written without lifting from the card what she always imagined as a stub of pencil-end studiously licked.

On the other side, their mother's name – Mrs Moss, with a grand M and a short stabbing line beneath the *rs* – then the address. Another warning down the edge, this time in smaller letters. 'The address only to be written on this side. If anything else is added, the postcard will be destroyed.' But across the top of her second card, Sammy had written something, and it had not been destroyed. A neat line of ink without the rough loopiness of his pencilled signature: '50 yds from the Germans. Posted from Trench.' In fifty years, one for each underlined yard, she had not come up with the answer. Why had he written it, why in ink, why had they allowed it? Sam was a cautious and responsible boy, especially towards their mother, and he would not have risked a worrying silence. But he had undeniably written these words. And in ink, too. Was it code for something else? A premonition of death? Except that Sam was not the sort to have premonitions. Perhaps it was simply excitement, a desire to impress. Look how close we are. 50 yds from the Germans. Posted from Trench.

She was glad he was at Cabaret Rouge, with his own headstone. Found and identified. Given known and honoured burial. She had a horror of Thiepval, one which failed to diminish in spite of her dutiful yearly visits. Thiepval's lost souls. You had to make the right preparation for them, for their lostness. So she always began elsewhere, at Caterpillar Valley, Thistle Dump, Quarry, Blighty Valley, Ulster Tower, Herbécourt.

> No Morning Dawns
> No Night Returns
> But What We Think Of Thee

That was at Herbécourt, a walled enclosure in the middle of fields, room for a couple of hundred, most of them Australian, but this was a British lad, the one who owned this inscription.

Was it a vice to have become such a connoisseur of grief? Yet it was true, she had her favourite cemeteries. Like Blighty Valley and Thistle Dump, both half-hidden from the road in a fold of valley; or Quarry, a graveyard looking as if it had been abandoned by its village; or Devonshire, that tiny, private patch for the Devonshires who died on the first day of the Somme, who fought to hold that ridge and held it still. You followed signposts in British racing green, then walked across fields guarded by wooden martyred Christs to these sanctuaries of orderliness, where everything was accounted for. Headstones were lined up like dominoes on edge; beneath them, their owners were present and correct, listed, tended. Creamy altars proclaimed that THEIR NAME LIVETH FOR EVERMORE. And so it did, on the graves, in the books, in hearts, in memories.

Each year she wondered if this would be her last visit. Her life no longer offered up to her the confident plausibility of two decades more, one decade, five years. Instead, it was now renewed on an annual basis, like her driving licence. Every April Dr Holling had to certify her fit for another twelve months behind the wheel. Perhaps she and the Morris would go kaput on the same day.

Before, it had been the boat train, the express to Amiens, a local stopper, a bus or two. Since she had acquired the Morris, she had in theory become freer; and yet her routine remained almost immutable. She would drive to Dover and take a night ferry, riding the Channel in the blackout alongside burly lorry-drivers. It saved money, and meant she was always in France for daybreak. No Morning Dawns . . . He must have seen each daybreak and wondered if that was the date they would put on his stone . . . Then she would follow the N43 to St-Omer, to Aire and Lillers, where she usually

94

took a croissant and *thé à l'anglaise*. From Lillers the N43 continued to Béthune, but she flinched from it: south of Béthune was the D937 to Arras, and there, on a straight stretch where the road did a reminding elbow, was Brigadier Sir Frank Higginson's domed portico. You should not drive past it, even if you intended to return. She had done that once, early in her ownership of the Morris, skirted Cabaret Rouge in second gear, and it had seemed the grossest discourtesy to Sammy and those who lay beside him: no, it's not your turn yet, just you wait and we'll be along. No, that was what the other motorists did.

So instead she would cut south from Lillers and come into Arras with the D341. From there, in that thinned triangle whose southern points were Albert and Péronne, she would begin her solemn and necessary tour of the woods and fields in which, so many decades before, the British Army had counter-attacked to relieve the pressure on the French at Verdun. That had been the start of it, anyway. No doubt scholars were by now having second thoughts, but that was what they were for; she herself no longer had arguments to deploy or positions to hold. She valued only what she had experienced at the time: an outline of strategy, the conviction of gallantry, and the facts of mourning.

At first, back then, the commonality of grief had helped: wives, mothers, comrades, an array of brass hats, and a bugler amid gassy morning mist which the feeble November sun had failed to burn away. Later, remembering Sam had changed: it became work, continuity; instead of anguish and glory, there was fierce unreasonableness, both about his death and her commemoration of it. During this period, she was hungry for the solitude and the voluptuous selfishness of grief: her Sam, her loss, her mourning, and nobody else's similar. She admitted as much: there was no shame to it. But now, after half a century, her feelings had simply become part of her. Her grief was a calliper, necessary and supporting; she could not imagine walking without it.

When she had finished with Herbécourt and Devonshire, Thistle Dump and Caterpillar Valley, she would come, always with trepidation, to the great red-brick memorial at Thiepval. An arch of triumph, yes, but of what kind, she wondered: the triumph over death, or the triumph *of* death? 'Here are recorded names of officers and men of the British armies who fell on the Somme battlefields July 1915–February 1918 but to whom the fortune of war denied the known and honoured burial given to their comrades in death.' Thiepval Ridge, Pozières Wood, Albert, Morval, Ginchy, Guillemont, Ancre, Ancre Heights, High Wood, Delville Wood, Bapaume, Bazentin Ridge, Miraumont, Transloy Ridges, Flers-Courcelette. Battle after battle, each accorded its stone laurel wreath, its section of wall: name after name after name, the Missing of the Somme, the official graffiti of death. This monument by Sir Edwin Lutyens revolted her, it always had. She could not bear the thought of these lost men, exploded into unrecognisable pieces, engulfed in the mud-fields, one moment fully there with pack and gaiters, baccy and rations, with their memories and their hopes, their past and their future, crammed into them, and the next moment only a shred of khaki or a sliver of shin-bone to prove they had ever existed. Or worse: some of these names had first been given known and honoured burial, their allotment of ground with their name above it, only for some new battle with its heedless artillery to tear up the temporary graveyard and bring a second, final extermination. Yet each of those scraps of uniform and flesh – whether newly killed or richly decomposed –

had been brought back here and reorganised, conscripted into the eternal regiment of the missing, kitted out and made to dress by the right. Something about the way they had vanished and the way they were now reclaimed was more than she could bear: as if an army which had thrown them away so lightly now chose to own them again so gravely. She was not sure whether this was the case. She claimed no understanding of military matters. All she claimed was an understanding of grief.

Her wariness of Thiepval always made her read it with a sceptical, a proof-reader's eye. She noticed, for instance, that the French translation of the English inscription listed – as the English one did not – the exact number of the Missing. 73,367. That was another reason she did not care to be here, standing in the middle of the arch looking down over the puny Anglo-French cemetery (French crosses to the left, British stones to the right) while the wind drew tears from an averting eye. 73,367: beyond a certain point, the numbers became uncountable and diminishing in effect. The more dead, the less proportionate the pain. 73,367: even she, with all her expertise in grief, could not imagine that.

Perhaps the British realised that the number of the Missing might continue to grow through the years, that no fixed total could be true; perhaps it was not shame, but a kind of sensible poetry which made them decline to specify a figure. And they were right: the numbers had indeed changed. The arch was inaugurated in 1932 by the Prince of Wales, and all the names of all the Missing had been carved upon its surfaces, but still, here and there, out of their proper place, hauled back tardily from oblivion, were a few soldiers enlisted only under the heading of Addenda. She knew all their names by now: Dodds T., Northumberland Fusiliers; Malcolm H. W.,

The Cameronians; Lennox F. J., Royal Irish Rifles; Lovell F. H. B., Royal Warwickshire Regiment; Orr R., Royal Inniskillins; Forbes R., Cameron Highlanders; Roberts J., Middlesex Regiment; Moxham A., Wiltshire Regiment; Humphries F. J., Middlesex Regiment; Hughes H. W., Worcestershire Regiment; Bateman W. T., Northamptonshire Regiment; Tarling E., The Cameronians; Richards W., Royal Field Artillery; Rollins S., East Lancashire Regiment; Byrne L., Royal Irish Rifles; Gale E. O., East Yorkshire Regiment; Walters J., Royal Fusiliers; Argar D., Royal Field Artillery. No Morning Dawns, No Night Returns . . .

She felt closest to Rollins S., since he was an East Lancashire; she would always smile at the initials inflicted upon Private Lovell; but it was Malcolm H. W. who used to intrigue her most. Malcolm H. W., or, to give him his full inscription: 'Malcolm H. W. The Cameronians (Sco. Rif.) served as Wilson H.' An addendum and a corrigendum all in one. When she had first discovered him, it had pleased her to imagine his story. Was he under age? Did he falsify his name to escape home, to run away from some girl? Was he wanted for a crime, like those fellows who joined the French Foreign Legion? She did not really want an answer, but she liked to dream a little about this man who had first been deprived of his identity and then of his life. These accumulations of loss seemed to exalt him; for a while, faceless and iconic, he had threatened to rival Sammy and Denis as an emblem of the war. In later years she turned against such fancifulness. There was no mystery really. Private H. W. Malcolm becomes H. Wilson. No doubt he was in truth H. Wilson Malcolm, and when he volunteered they wrote the wrong name in the wrong column; then they were unable to change it. That would make sense: man is only a clerical error corrected by death.

She had never cared for the main inscription over the central arch:

AUX ARMEES
FRANCAISE ET
BRITANNIQUE
L'EMPIRE
BRITANNIQUE
RECON-
NAISSANT

Each line was centred, which was correct, but there was altogether too much white space beneath the inscription. She would have inserted 'less #' on the galley-proof. And each year she disliked more and more the line-break in the word *reconnaissant*. There were different schools of thought about this – she had argued with her superiors over the years – but she insisted that breaking a word in the middle of a doubled consonant was a nonsense. You broke a word where the word itself was perforated. Look what this military, architectural or sculptural nincompoop had produced: a fracture which left a separate word, *naissant*, by mistake. *Naissant* had nothing to do with *reconnaissant*, nothing at all; worse, it introduced the notion of birth on to this monument to death. She had written to the War Graves Commission about it, many years ago, and had been assured that the proper procedures had been followed. They told *her* that!

Nor was she content with EVERMORE. Their name liveth for evermore: here at Thiepval, also at Cabaret Rouge, Caterpillar Valley, Combles Communal Cemetery Extension, and all the larger memorials. It was of course the correct form, or at least the more regular form; but something in her preferred to see it as two words. EVER MORE: it seemed more weighty like this, with an equal bell-toll on each half. In any case, she had a quarrel with the Dictionary about *evermore*. 'Always, at all times, constantly, continually'. Yes, it could mean this in the ubiquitous inscription. But she preferred sense 1: 'For all future time'. Their name liveth for all future time. No morning dawns, no night returns, but what we think of thee. This is what the inscription meant. But the Dictionary had marked sense 1 as '*Obs. exc. arch.*' Obsolete except archaic. No, oh certainly not, no. And not with a last quotation as recent as 1854. She would have spoken to Mr Rothwell about this, or at least pencilled a looping note on the galley-proof; but this entry was not being revised, and the letter E had passed over her desk without an opportunity to make the adjustment.

EVERMORE. She wondered if there was such a thing as collective memory, something more than the sum of individual memories. If so, was it merely coterminous, yet in some way richer; or did it last longer? She wondered if those too young to have original knowledge could be given memory, could have it grafted on. She thought of this especially at Thiepval. Though she hated the place, when she saw young families trailing across the grass towards the red-brick *arc-de-triomphe* it also roused in her a wary hopefulness. Christian cathedrals could inspire religious faith by their vast assertiveness; why then should not Lutyens' memorial provoke some response equally beyond the rational? That reluctant child, whining about the strange food its mother produced from plastic boxes, might receive memory here. Such an edifice assured the newest eye of the pre-existence of the profoundest emotions. Grief and awe lived here; they could be breathed, absorbed. And if so, then this child might in turn bring its child, and so on, from generation to generation, EVERMORE. Not just to count the Missing, but to understand what those from whom they had gone missing knew, and to feel her loss afresh.

Perhaps this was one reason she had married Denis. Of course she should never have done so. And in a way she never had, for there had been no carnal connection: she unwilling, he incapable. It had lasted two years and his uncomprehending eyes when she delivered him back were impossible to forget. All she could say in her defence was that it was the only time she had behaved with such pure selfishness: she had married him for her own reasons, and discarded him for her own reasons. Some might say that the rest of her life had been selfish too, devoted as it was entirely to her own commemorations; but this was a selfishness that hurt nobody else.

Poor Denis. He was still handsome when he came back, though his hair grew white on one side and he dribbled. When the fits came on she knelt on his chest and held his tongue down with a stub of pencil. Every night he roamed restlessly through his sleep, muttered and roared, fell silent for a while, and then with parade-ground precision would shout *Hip! hip! hip!* When she woke him, he could never remember what had been happening. He had guilt and pain, but no specific memory of what he felt guilty about. She knew: Denis had been hit by shrapnel and taken back down the line to hospital without a farewell to his best pal Jewy Moss, leaving Sammy to be killed during the next day's Hun bombardment. After two years of this marriage, two years of watching Denis vigorously brush his patch of white hair to make it go away, she had returned him to his sisters. From now on, she told them, they should look after Denis and she would look after Sam. The sisters had gazed at her in silent astonishment. Behind them, in the hall, Denis, his chin wet and his brown eyes uncomprehending, stood with an awkward patience which implied that this latest event was nothing special in itself, merely one of a number of things he failed to grasp, and that there would surely be much more to come, all down the rest of his life, which would also escape him.

She had taken the job on the Dictionary a month later. She worked alone in a damp basement, at a desk across which curled long sheets of galley-proof. Condensation beaded the window. She was armed with a brass table-lamp and a pencil which she sharpened until it was too short to fit in the hand. Her script was large and loose, somewhat like Sammy's; she deleted and inserted, just as he had done on his field-service postcards. Nothing to be written on this side of the galley-proof. If anything else is added to the galley-proof it will be destroyed. No, she did not have to worry; she made her marks with impunity. She spotted colons which were italic instead of roman, brackets which were square instead of round, inconsistent abbreviations, misleading cross-references. Occasionally she made suggestions. She might observe, in looping pencil, that such-and-such a word was in her opinion vulgar rather than colloquial, or that the sense illustrated was figurative rather than transferred. She passed on her galley-proofs to Mr Rothwell, the joint deputy editor, but never enquired whether her annotations were finally acted upon. Mr Rothwell, a bearded, taciturn and pacific man, valued her meticulous eye, her sure grasp of the Dictionary's conventions, and her willingness to take work home if a fascicle was shortly going to press. He remarked to himself and to others that she had a strangely disputatious attitude over words labelled as obsolete. Often she would propose *?Obs.* rather than *Obs.* as the correct marking. Perhaps this had something to do with age, Mr Rothwell thought; younger folk were perhaps more willing to accept that a word had had its day.

In fact, Mr Rothwell was only five years younger than she; but Miss Moss — as she had become once more after her disposal of Denis — had aged quickly, almost as a matter of will. The years passed and she grew stout, her hair flew a little more wildly away from her clips, and her spectacle lenses became thicker. Her stockings had a dense, antique look to them, and she never took her raincoat to the dry-cleaner. Younger lexicographers entering her office, where a number of back files were stored, wondered if the faint smell of rabbit-hutch came from the walls, the old Dictionary slips, Miss Moss's raincoat, or Miss Moss herself. None of this mattered to Mr Rothwell, who saw only the precision of her work. Though entitled by the Press to an annual holiday of fifteen working days, she never took more than a single week.

At first this holiday coincided with the eleventh hour of the eleventh day of the eleventh month; Mr Rothwell had the delicacy not to ask for details. In later years, however, she would take her week in other months, late spring or early autumn. When her parents died and she inherited a small amount of money, she surprised Mr Rothwell by arriving for work one day in a small grey Morris with red leather seats. It sported a yellow metal AA badge on the front and a metal GB plate on the back. At the age of fifty-three she had passed her driving-test first time, and manoeuvred her car with a precision bordering on elan.

She always slept in the car. It saved money; but mainly

it helped her be alone with herself and Sam. The villages in that thinned triangle south of Arras became accustomed to the sight of an ageing British car the colour of gunmetal drawn up beside the war memorial; inside, an elderly lady wrapped in a travelling-rug would be asleep in the passenger seat. She never locked the car at night, for it seemed impertinent, even disrespectful on her part to feel any fear. She slept while the villages slept, and would wake as a drenched cow on its way to milking softly shouldered a wing of the parked Morris. Every so often she would be invited in by a villager, but she preferred not to accept hospitality. Her behaviour was not regarded as peculiar, and cafés in the region knew to serve her *thé à l'anglaise* without her having to ask.

After she had finished with Thiepval, with Thistle Dump and Caterpillar Valley, she would drive up through Arras and take the D937 towards Béthune. Ahead lay Vimy, Cabaret Rouge, N.D. de Lorette. But there was always one other visit to be paid first: to Maison Blanche. Such peaceful names they mostly had. But here at Maison Blanche were 40,000 German dead, 40,000 Huns laid out beneath their thin black crosses, a sight as orderly as you would expect from the Huns, though not as splendid as the British graves. She lingered there, reading a few names at random, idly wondering, when she found a date just a little later than the 21st January 1917, if this could be the Hun that had killed her Sammy. Was this the man who squeezed the trigger, fed the machine-gun, blocked his ears as the howitzer roared? And see how short a time he had lasted afterwards: two days, a week, a month or so in the mud before being lined up in known and honoured burial, facing out once more towards her Sammy, though separated now not by barbed-wire and 50 yds but by a few kilometres of asphalt.

She felt no rancour towards these Huns; time had washed from her any anger at the man, the regiment, the Hun army, the nation that had taken Sam's life. Her resentment was against those who had come later, and whom she refused to dignify with the amicable name of Hun. She hated Hitler's war for diminishing the memory of the Great War, for allotting it a number, the mere first among two. And she hated the way in which the Great War was held responsible for its successor, as if Sam, Denis and all the East Lancashires who fell were partly the cause of that business. Sam had done what he could – he had served and died – and was punished all too quickly with becoming subservient in memory. Time did not behave rationally. Fifty years back to the Somme; a hundred beyond that to Waterloo; four hundred more to Agincourt, or Azincourt as the French preferred. Yet these distances had now been squeezed closer to one another. She blamed it on 1939–1945.

She knew to keep away from those parts of France where the second war happened, or at least where it was remembered. In the early years of the Morris, she had sometimes made the mistake of imagining herself on holiday, of being a tourist. She might thoughtlessly stop in a lay-by, or be taking a stroll down a back lane in some tranquil, heat-burdened part of the country, when a neat tablet inserted in a dry wall would assault her. It would commemorate Monsieur Un Tel, *lâchement assassiné par les Allemands*, or *tué*, or *fusillé*, and then an insulting modern date: 1943, 1944, 1945. They blocked the view, these deaths and these dates; they demanded attention by their recency. She refused, she refused.

When she stumbled like this upon the second war, she would hurry to the nearest village for consolation. She always knew where to look: next to the church, the *mairie*, the railway station; at a fork in the road; on a dusty square with cruelly pollarded limes and a few rusting café tables. There she would find her damp-stained memorial with its heroic *poilu*, grieving widow, triumphant Marianne, rowdy cockerel. Not that the story she read on the plinth needed any sculptural illustration. 67 against 9, 83 against 12, 40 against 5, 27 against 2: here was the eternal corroboration she sought, the historical corrigendum. She would touch the names cut into stone, their gilding washed away on the weather-side. Numbers whose familiar proportion declared the terrible primacy of the Great War. Her eye would check down the bigger list, snagging at a name repeated twice, thrice, four, five, six times: one male generation of an entire family taken away to known and honoured burial. In the bossy statistics of death she would find the comfort she needed.

She would spend the last night at Aix-Noulette (101 to 7); at Souchez (48 to 6), where she remembered Plouvier, Maxime, Sergent, killed on 17th December 1916, the last of his village to die before her Sam; at Carency (19 to 1); at Ablain-Saint-Nazaire (66 to 9), eight of whose male Lherbiers had died, four on the *champ d'honneur*, three as *victimes civiles*, one a *civil fusillé par l'ennemi*. Then, the next morning, cocked with grief, she would set off for Cabaret Rouge while dew was still on the grass. There was consolation in solitude and damp knees. She no longer talked to Sam; everything had been said decades ago. The heart had been expressed, the apologies made, the secrets given. She no longer wept, either; that too had stopped. But the hours she spent with him at Cabaret Rouge were the most vital of her life. They always had been.

The D937 did its reminding elbow at Cabaret Rouge, making sure you slowed out of respect, drawing your attention to Brigadier Sir Frank Higginson's handsome domed portico, which served as both entrance gate and memorial arch. From the portico, the burial ground dropped away at first, then sloped up again towards the standing cross on which hung not Christ but a metal sword. Symmetrical, amphitheatrical, Cabaret Rouge held 6,676 British soldiers, sailors, Marines and airmen; 732 Canadians; 121 Australians; 42 South Africans; 7 New Zealanders; 2 members of the Royal Guernsey Light Infantry; 1 Indian; 1 member of an unknown unit; and 4 Germans.

It also contained, or more exactly had once had scattered over it, the ashes of Brigadier Sir Frank Higginson, Secretary to the Imperial War Graves Commission, who had died in 1958 at the age of sixty-eight. That showed true loyalty and remembrance. His widow, Lady Violet Lindsley Higginson, had died four years later, and her ashes had been scattered here too. Fortunate Lady Higginson. Why should the wife of a brigadier who, whatever he had done in the Great War, had not died, be allowed such enviable and meritorious burial, and yet the sister of one of those soldiers whom the fortune of war had led to known and honoured burial be denied such comfort? The Commission had twice denied her request, saying that a military cemetery did not receive civilian ashes. The third time she had written they had been less polite, referring her brusquely to their earlier correspondence.

There had been incidents down the years. They had stopped her coming for the eleventh hour of the eleventh day of the eleventh month by refusing her permission to sleep the night beside his grave. They said they did not have camping facilities; they affected to sympathise, but what if everybody else wanted to do the same? She replied that it was quite plain that no one else wanted to do the same but that if they did then such a desire should be respected. However, after some years she ceased to miss the official ceremony: it seemed to her full of people who remembered improperly, impurely.

There had been problems with the planting. The grass at the cemetery was French grass, and it seemed to her of the coarser type, inappropriate for British soldiers to lie beneath. Her campaign over this with the Commission led nowhere. So one spring she took out a small spade and a square yard of English turf kept damp in a plastic bag. After dark she dug out the offending French grass and relaid the softer English turf, patting it into place, then stamping it in. She was pleased with her work, and the next year, as she approached the grave, saw no indication of her mending. But when she knelt, she realised that her work had been undone: the French grass was back again. The same had happened when she had surreptitiously planted her bulbs. Sam liked tulips, yellow ones especially, and one autumn she had pushed half a dozen bulbs into the earth. But the following spring, when she returned, there were only dusty geraniums in front of his stone.

There had also been the desecration. Not so very long ago. Arriving shortly after dawn, she found something on the grass which at first she put down to a dog. But when she saw the same in front of 1685 Private W. A. Andrade 4th Bn. London Regt. R. Fus. 15th March 1915, and in front of 675 Private Leon Emanuel Levy The Cameronians (Sco. Rif.) 16th August 1916 aged 21 And the Soul Returneth to God Who Gave It – Mother, she judged it most unlikely that a dog, or three dogs, had managed to find the only three Jewish graves in the cemetery. She gave the caretaker the rough edge of her tongue. He admitted that such desecration had occurred before, also that paint had been sprayed, but he always tried to arrive before anyone else and remove the signs. She told him that he might be honest but he was clearly idle. She blamed the second war. She tried not to think about it again.

For her, now, the view back to 1917 was uncluttered: the decades were mown grass, and at their end was a row of white headstones, domino-thin. 1358 Private Samuel M. Moss East Lancashire Regt. 21st January 1917, and in the middle the Star of David. Some graves in Cabaret Rouge were anonymous, with no identifying words or symbols; some had inscriptions, regimental badges, Irish harps, springboks, maple leaves, New Zealand ferns. Most had Christian crosses; only three displayed the Star of David. Private Andrade, Private Levy and Private Moss. A British soldier buried beneath the Star of David: she kept her eyes on that. Sam had written from training camp that the fellows chaffed him, but he had always been Jewy Moss at school, and they were good fellows, most of them, as good inside the barracks as outside, anyway. They made the same remarks he'd heard before, but Jewy Moss was a British soldier, good enough to fight and die with his comrades, which is what he had done, and what he was remembered for. She pushed away the second war, which muddled things. He was a British soldier, East Lancashire Regiment, buried at Cabaret Rouge beneath the Star of David.

She wondered when they would plough them up, Herbé-court, Devonshire, Quarry, Blighty Valley, Ulster Tower, Thistle Dump and Caterpillar Valley; Maison Blanche and Cabaret Rouge. They said they never would. This land, she read everywhere, was 'the free gift of the French people for the perpetual resting place of those of the allied armies who fell . . .' and so on. EVERMORE, they said, and she wanted to hear: for all future time. The War Graves Commission, her successive members of parliament, the Foreign Office, the commanding officer of Sammy's regiment, all told her the same. She didn't believe them. Soon – in fifty years or so – everyone who had served in the War would be dead; and at some point after that, everyone who had known anyone who had served would also be dead. What if memory-grafting did not work, or the memories themselves were deemed shameful? First, she guessed, those little stone tablets in the back lanes would be chiselled out, since the French and the Germans had officially stopped hating one another years ago, and it would not do for German tourists to be accused of the cowardly assassinations perpetrated by their ancestors. Then the war memorials would come down, with their important statistics. A few might be held to have architectural interest; but some new, cheerful generation would find them morbid, and dream up better things to enliven the villages. And after that it would be time to plough up the cemeteries, to put them back to good agricultural use: they had lain fallow for too long. Priests and politicians would make it all right, and the farmers would get their land back, fertilised with blood and bone. Thiepval might become a listed building, but would they keep Brigadier Sir Frank Higginson's domed portico? That elbow in the D937 would be declared a traffic hazard; all it needed was a drunken casualty for the road to be made straight again after all these years. Then the great forgetting could begin, the fading into the landscape. The war would be levelled to a couple of museums, a set of demonstration trenches, and a few names, shorthand for pointless sacrifice.

Might there be one last fiery glow of remembering? In her own case, it would not be long before her annual renewals ceased, before the clerical error of her life was corrected; yet even as she pronounced herself an antique, her memories seemed to sharpen. If this happened to the individual, could it not also happen on a national scale? Might there not be, at some point in the first decades of the twenty-first century, one final moment, lit by evening sun, before the whole thing was handed over to the archivists? Might there not be a great looking-back down the mown grass of the decades, might not a gap in the trees discover the curving ranks of slender headstones, white tablets holding up to the eye their bright names and terrifying dates, their harps and springboks, maple leaves and ferns, their Christian crosses and their Stars of David? Then, in the space of a wet blink, the gap in the trees would close and the mown grass disappear, a violent indigo cloud would cover the sun, and history, gross history, daily history, would forget. Is this how it would be?

# GNOSSIENNE

○

L ET ME MAKE IT CLEAR that I never attend literary
conferences. I know that they're held in art deco hotels
close to legendary museums; that sessions on the future
of the novel are conducted with *Kameradschaft, brio* and *bon-
homie*; that the impromptu friendships always endure; and that
after the work is done you may savour hard liquor, soft drugs
and a fair slither of sex. Taxi-drivers in Frankfurt are said to
dislike the annual Book Fair because literary folk, instead of
being shuttled to prostitutes like respectable members of other
convening professions, prefer to stay in their hotels and fuck
one another. I also know that literary conferences are held in
mafia-built blocks whose air-conditioning throbs with
typhoid, tetanus and diphtheria; that the organisers are inter-
national snobs seeking local tax write-offs; that delegates covet
the free air-ticket and the chance to bore their rivals in several
different languages simultaneously; that in the presumed
democracy of art everyone acknowledges and consequently
resents their place in the true hierarchy; and that not a single
novelist, poet, essayist or even journalist has ever left that mafia
hotel a better writer than he or she entered it. I know all
this, as I say, because I have never attended a single literary
conference.

My replies are sent on postcards free of my own address:

'Sorry, no'; 'Don't do conferences'; 'Regret travelling elsewhere in the world'; and so on. The opening line of my
reply to French invitations was not perfected for some years.
Eventually it became: *'Je regrette que je ne suis pas conférencier ni
de tempérament ni d'aptitude . . .'* I was rather pleased with this:
if I pleaded mere incapacity it might be read as modesty,
and if I pleaded temperamental unsuitability alone, conditions
might be improved until it would be too difficult for me to
refuse. This way I had rendered myself invulnerable to any
comeback.

It was the sheer amateurishness of the invitation to Marrant that made me read it twice. Perhaps I don't mean amateurish; more old-fashioned, as if it came from a vanished world.
There was no municipal seal, no promise of five-star accom-
modation, no menu-list for S&M devotees of literary theory.
The paper was unheaded, and though the signature looked
original, the text above it had that faded, blurry, purply look
of the Roneo machine or pre-war carbon paper. Some of the
letters on the original typewriter (clearly an old manual, with
sticky-up keys for a single-finger operator to peck at) were
cracked. I noted all this; but what I most noted – what made
me wonder briefly if I might for once have the temperament
and the aptitude – was the sentence which stood by itself
above the signature. The main text explained that the conference would take place in a certain small village in the Massif
Central on a particular day in October. My presence would
be welcome but a reply was not expected; I merely had to
arrive by one of the three trains listed overleaf. Then came
the statement of intent, opaque, whimsical, seductive: 'The
point of the conference consists in being met at the station:
attendance is performance.'

I checked the letter again. No, I wasn't being asked to

give a paper, sit on a panel, fret about Whither the Novel. I wasn't being wooed with an A-list of fellow *conférenciers*. I wasn't being offered my fare, my hotel bill, let alone a fee. I frowned at the looping signature untranslated into type. There was something familiar about it, which I eventually located, as I did the insouciance and cheeky familiarity of the invitation, in a particular French literary tradition: Jarry, pataphysics, Queneau, Perec, the OULIPO group and so on. The official unofficials, the honoured rebels. Jean-Luc Cazes, yes, surely he was one of that gang. A bit of a surprise that he was still alive. What was that definition of pataphysics? 'The science of imagining solutions.' And the point of the conference consisted in being met at the station.

I didn't have to reply: this, I think, was what enchanted me. I didn't have to say whether I was going or not. So the letter was lost and rediscovered among that sticky scatter of bills and receipts, invitations and VAT forms, proofs, begging letters and PLR print-outs which habitually shrouds my desk. One afternoon I got out the appropriate yellow Michelin map: no. 76. There it was: Marrant-sur-Cère, thirty or forty kilometres short of Aurillac. The railway line from Clermont-Ferrand ran straight through the village, whose name, I noticed, wasn't underlined in red. So no listing in the Michelin guide. I double-checked, in case my yellow map was out of date, but there was no entry, nor one in the *Logis de France* either. Where would they put me up? This wasn't a part of the Cantal I was familiar with. I grazed the map for a few minutes, making it work like a pop-up book: steep hill, *point de vue*, hikers' trail, *maison forestière*. I imagined chestnut groves, truffle-hounds, forest clearings where charcoal-makers had once practised. Small mahogany cows jigged on the slopes of extinct volcanoes to the music of local bagpipes. I imagined all this, because my actual memories of the Cantal reduced to two items: cheese and rain.

The English autumn succumbed to the first spiky prod of winter; fallen leaves were sugar-dusted by early frost. I flew to Clermont-Ferrand and stayed the night at the Albert-Elisabeth (*sans restaurant*). At the station the next morning, I did as I had been told: I booked a ticket to Vic-sur-Cère without mentioning to the clerk that my actual destination was Marrant. Certain trains – the three listed on my invitation – would stop at Marrant, but they would do so exceptionally, and by private arrangement with certain individuals connected with the railway. This touch of mystery pleased me: I felt a spy's relish when the departures board showed no intermediate stop between Murat and Vic-sur-Cère. I had only hand-luggage anyway: the train would slow as if for a routine red light, would pause, squeak, exhale, and in that moment I would make a goblin disembarkation, shutting the door with a sly caress. If anyone saw me get off, they would assume I was an SNCF employee being done a favour by the driver.

I had been imagining some old-fashioned French train, the ferrovial equivalent of the Roneoed invitation, but I found myself in a smartly-liveried, four-carriage job with driver-controlled doors. I updated my descent at Marrant: I would rise from my seat as we left Murat, stand casually close to the door, wait for the conspiratorial humph of compressed air and be gone before the other passengers could miss me. I managed the first part of the manoeuvre without trouble; ostentatiously casual, I didn't even look through the glass as the anticipated deceleration finally took hold. The train stopped, the doors opened and I got off. To my surprise I was hustled from behind by what logically I took to be other *conférenciers* – except that they were two broad-hipped, headscarfed women

of uplands rubicundity whom you would expect to see behind
a trestle table selling twelve eggs and a skinned rabbit rather
than signing copies of their latest novel. My second surprise
was to read the words VIC-SUR-CÈRE. Shit! I must have been
dreaming – my station must be after Vic, not before. I scooted
back between the humphing doors and pulled out my invitation. Shit again! I'd been right the first time. So much for
private arrangements with certain individuals. The bloody
driver had gone straight through Marrant. Obviously no taste
for literature, that fellow. I was swearing, and yet in a remarkably good mood.

At Aurillac I hired a car and took the N126 back up the
Cère valley. I passed through Vic, and began looking out for
a D-road east to Marrant. The weather was closing in, a fact
I noted with benign neutrality. Normally I'm intolerant of
fuck-ups: I find that enough things go wrong at my desk
without more going wrong in all the contingent aspects of
the literary life. The inert microphone at a public reading; the
self-erasing tape-recorder; the journalist whose questions fail
to fit any of the answers you might be capable of fabricating
in an entire lifetime. I once did an interview for French
radio in a Paris hotel room. There was a sound-check, the
recordist pressed the switch and, as the spools began to circle,
the interviewer shaved my chin with the microphone. 'Monsieur Clements,' he asked, with a kind of intimate authority,
'le mythe et la réalité?' I stared at him for quite some time,
feeling my French evaporate and my brain dry. Eventually, I
gave him the only answer I could: that such questions and
their appropriate responses no doubt came naturally to French
intellectuals, but that since I was a mere pragmatic English
novelist, he would get a better interview out of me if he
perhaps approached such larger matters by way of smaller,

lighter ones. This would also, I explained, help warm up my French for me. He smiled in concord, the engineer wound back the tape and the microphone was placed again like a tear-glass to catch my drops of wisdom. 'Monsieur Clements, we are sitting here in your hotel room in Paris one afternoon in April. The window is open, and outside is unrolling the daily life of the city. Opposite the window is a wardrobe with a tall mirror in the door. I look in the wardrobe mirror and in it I can almost see reflected the daily life of Paris which is unrolling outside the window. Monsieur Clements, *le mythe et la réalité?*'

The D-road climbed sharply towards a barrier of high mist or low cloud. I switched on my windscreen-wipers in anticipation; then twisted the headlights to full beam, prodded the fog-lamp, wound the window down a little and chuckled. What an absurd idea to escape from an English October to one of the wettest parts of France: like the American who saw the Second World War coming and relocated to Guadalcanal. Visibility was no more than a few metres, the road was narrow, and on the nearside the ground dropped away into the unknown. Through my half-open window I thought I heard cowbells, a goat and the squeal of bagpipes, unless it was just a pig. My mood continued to be one of cheerful certainty. I didn't feel like an anxious tourist groping for a destination; more a confident writer who knows where his book is going.

I came out of wet mist into sudden sunlight and a sky of Ingres blue. The village of Marrant was deserted: the shops had their shutters down; the trays of vegetables outside the *épicerie* were covered with sacking; a dog snoozed on a doorstep. The church clock showed 2.50 but creakily struck three as I looked. The *boulangerie* had its opening hours engraved into the glass of its door: 8h-12h, 16h-19h. It made me feel nostalgic: these old-fashioned timings had ruled when I first discovered France. If you hadn't bought your picnic lunch by twelve you went hungry, because everyone knew that in French villages the *charcutier* has to take four hours off to sleep with the baker's wife, the baker four hours to sleep with the owner of the *quincaillerie*, and so on. As for Mondays: forget it. Everything would shut down from Sunday lunchtime to Tuesday morning. Now the pan-European commercial impulse had reached everywhere in France, except, oddly, here.

The station also had a lunchtime look as I approached it. The booking-office and newsagent's kiosk were both closed, though for some reason the public-address system seemed to be broadcasting music. An amateurish brass band oompahing away: Scott Joplin by the sound of it. I pushed open a grimy glass door, turned on to an unswept platform, noticed thistles growing between the sleepers and saw, to my left, a small welcoming party. A mayor, or at least a man looking like a mayor, from sash of office to chinstrap beard. Behind him was the most peculiar municipal band I had ever seen: one cornet, one tuba and a serpent, all going hard at the same bit of ragtime, music-hall or whatever. The mayor, young, plumpish and sallow, stepped forward, grasped my upper arms and gave me a ceremonial two-cheek kiss.

'Thank you for meeting me,' I said automatically.

'Attendance is performance,' he replied, smiling. 'We hope you are pleased to hear the music of your country.'

'I'm not American, I'm afraid.'

'Nor was Satie,' said the mayor. 'Ah, you didn't know that his mother was Scottish? Well. The piece is called "Le Piccadilly". Shall we continue?'

For some reason unknown to myself yet approved by the

mayor, I fell in directly behind him and kept step as he led the way. Behind me the *ad hoc* trio struck up 'Le Piccadilly' again. I got to know the piece pretty well, since it lasts just over a minute and they played it seven or eight times as we processed down the platform, over an unguarded level-crossing and through the dormant town. I expected the *charcutier* to protest that the brassy blast was affecting his sexual concentration with the baker's wife, or at least an inquisitive urchin to speed out of a shady alley-way, but we passed only a few inert pets, who behaved as if this three o'clock concert was normal. Not a shutter stirred.

The village petered out by a lilting *lavoir*, a humpy bridge and a spread of immaculate but untenanted allotments. An old Citroën appeared from nowhere and suavely overtook us. You don't see many of those cars any more: you know, the black ones that sit wide and hippy on the road, running-boards at the side, Maigret at the wheel. But I didn't spot the driver as he disappeared in a dusty curve.

We passed the cemetery, with my backing group still pomping out 'Le Piccadilly'. A high wall, the steeply prongs of a few plutocratic tombs, then a quick view through a chained gate. Sun flashed on glass: I had forgotten the custom of building little greenhouses over and around the tombs. Is it symbolic protection for the departed, self-interest for the mourners, or simply a way of ensuring fresh flowers for a longer season? I never found a gravedigger to ask. In any case, you don't really want answers to every question. About your own country, perhaps. But about others? Leave some space for reverie, for amical invention.

We halted outside the gates of a small manor-house of proportions laid down by God. Biscuity stone, thunder-grey slate roof, modest pepper-pot towers at each corner.

A venerable wisteria in its miraculous second flowering hung over a front door reached by double-sided steps which no doubt had once served as a mounting-block. The mayor and I now walked side by side across the gravel, our feet inciting a distant, unthreatening bark from the stables. Behind the house were some rising beech woods; to the left a shaded pond with several varieties of edible wildlife; beyond that, a sloping meadow eased towards the sort of lush valley that the British would convert into a golf-course. I stopped; the mayor propelled me forward by an elbow. I climbed two steps, paused to inhale the wisteria blossom, climbed six more, turned and saw that he had disappeared. I was not in the mood to be surprised – or rather, what would normally have surprised me struck me as perfectly understandable. In ordinary, pedantic life I might have asked myself at what precise point the band had stopped playing, whether the Maigret Citroën was garaged in the stables, why I hadn't heard the mayor's feet on the gravel. Instead, I merely thought, I am here, they are gone. Normally, I would have tugged on the bell-pull which hung down through a rusty, iron ring; instead I pushed the door.

Part of me expected a bobbing chambermaid with gauffred mob-cap and an apron tied in the middle of her arching back with a floppy double bow. Instead, I found some more purply Roneoed words informing me that my room was at the top of the stairs and that I would be expected in the *salon* at seven-thirty. The boards creaked, as I knew they would, in a comforting rather than sinister fashion. The shutters of my room were propped half-open, giving enough light for me to take in the jug and bowl on a marble washstand, the brass bedstead, the curvy armoire. A Bonnard interior, lacking only a cat, or perhaps Mme Bonnard sponging herself in the bathroom. I lay on the bed and hovered halfway to sleep, untempted by dreams, unperturbed by reality.

How can I describe the sense of being there, in that village, in that room, the familiarity of it all? It was not, as you might think, the familiarity of memory. The best way I can explain it is to make a literary comparison, which seems fair enough in the circumstances. Gide once said that he wrote in order to be reread. Some years ago I interviewed the novelist Michel Tournier, who quoted me this line, paused and added with a certain smiling complacency, 'Whereas *I* write to be reread on the first occasion.' Do you see what I mean?

Downstairs at seven-thirty, I was greeted by Jean-Luc Cazes, one of those old-fashioned, Left-Bank, anarcho-rock characters (tired leather blouson, pipe wedged in the corner of mouth), the sort of genial zinc-bar philosopher you suspect has an alarming success rate among women. Handing me a *vin blanc* so viscous with cassis as to arouse the suspicion that Canon Kir must have had a lot of inferior white wine on his hands, he introduced me to the other guests: a Spanish poet, an Algerian film-maker, an Italian semiotician, a Swiss crime-writer, a German dramatist and a Belgian art critic. Cazes was fluent in all our languages, though we each spoke French more or less approximately. I meant to ask the others about their invitations, their arrivals, their receptions, their tunes, but somehow it never came to that; or if it did, I have forgotten.

Dinner was served by a shy peasant girl with high, nasal vowels, her *a* moving towards *i*: 'Si vous n'ivez pas suffisimint, vous n'ivez qu'à deminder,' she told us with nervous authority. A thick, cabbagy, ham-bony soup which I imagined snoring gently in a large copper for five days or so. A tomato salad with a vinegary dressing. An omelette *aux fines herbes* which ran *baveuse* when you put the spoon into it. A plate of pink *gigot* with gravy like thinned blood. Round, big-beaned *haricots verts* cooked until floppy, and drenched in butter. Salad. Four types of cheese. A fruit bowl. Wine in unlabelled litre bottles with a row of stars across the shoulder like an American general. Cutlery handed down from course to course. Coffee and a *vieille prune*.

We talked easily: this was not, after all, a conference, and M. Cazes was less *animateur* than encouraging presence. The others . . . you know, I can't remember what they said, though at the time it made sense to me, especially in the light of what I knew, or thought I knew, about their reputations. For myself, I discovered an improbable spontaneity when my turn came to address the table. I had, of course, prepared nothing, secure in the promise that attendance was performance; yet I eased into a confident *tour d'horizon* of various French cultural topics, and managed strangely well. I talked about *Le Grand Meaulnes, Le Petit Prince*, Greuze, Astérix, the *comédie larmoyante*, Bernardin de Saint-Pierre, pre-Great War railway posters, Rousseau, Offenbach, the early films of Fernandel and the semiotic significance of the yellow triangular – nay, tricornic – Ricard ashtray. You should understand that this is not how I normally behave. I have a poor memory and little capacity for generalisation. I prefer to discuss a single book, or better still a single chapter, or best of all a single page which I happen to have in front of me.

I told them a story to illustrate what I meant by Gallic charm. I once appeared on 'Apostrophes', the television book programme, with a French novelist who had written the autobiography of his cat. He was a well-known writer who had unhooked several domestic literary prizes. When the host asked him about the composition of his latest work, he replied, 'I did not write the book, my cat wrote the book.' This response irritated the host, who began attacking the novelist. 'I did not write the book,' he replied every time, a Gauloise smokescreening his white polo-necked sweater and mustachioed smile. 'My cat wrote the book.' We all chuckled at this example of whimsical provocation.

I'd better warn you that there was no *coup*. No sudden electrical storm across a midnight sky, no *feux d'artifice* or irruption of mime artists. No one walked, arm mythically extended, towards a full-length mirror, vanishing into and beyond it; there were no *visiteurs du soir*. Nor was there a *coup* in the French sense: no flamboyant episode with svelte *conférencière* or tangy servant-girl; Mme Bonnard did not get out of her bath for me. We went to bed early after shaking hands all round.

Cheese is supposed to provoke bad dreams, but the combination of Brie, Saint-Nectaire and Pont-l'Evèque (I had declined the Bon Bel) had the opposite effect. I slept eventlessly, without even one of those tranquil episodes in which someone whom I knew to be me yet was not moved across landscapes both strange and familiar towards a reward both surprising yet predictable. I woke clear-headed to the sound of a late-season bumble-bee butting against the peeling slats of the shutters. Downstairs, I dipped my still-warm baguette into my bowl of hot chocolate and set off for the station before the others were up. Dewy spiders' webs caught the early-morning sun like Christmas decorations. I heard a clattering behind me and was overtaken by one of those itinerant butcher's vans made from silvery corrugated metal. At the station I picked up my car and drove through the village which seemed dormant, though I could see that the pavement in front of the shops had already been sluiced and broomed. It was 7.40 and the creaky church clock struck the three-quarter.

When I started the car, my headlights and wipers came on, and I soon needed both as I headed down through damp morning mist to rejoin the N126. At Aurillac, another smart, four-carriage train was ready to take me to Clermont-Ferrand. There were few passengers, and my view was unimpeded; at times, I could even see the N126, which helped locate me. We stopped at Vic-sur-Cère and thereafter I paid particular attention. I was apprehensive about that misty cloud, but the soft October sun must have burnt it off. I watched, I switched my head regularly from side to side, I listened out for the train's warning whistle, and all I can say is that we didn't pass through the station of Marrant-sur-Cère.

As the plane ended its first curving climb, and the levelling wing erased the Puy-de-Dôme, I remembered the name of the French writer who had written the autobiography of his cat. I also remembered my reaction as I sat next to him in the studio: you pretentious twat, I thought, or some such words. The French writers I am loyal to run from Montaigne to Voltaire to Flaubert to Mauriac to Camus. Does it need saying that I am unable to read *Le Petit Prince* and find most of Greuze nauseating? I am sentimental about clarity of thought, emotional about rationality.

When I was an adolescent I used to come to France with my parents for motoring holidays. I had never seen a Bonnard. The only cheese I would eat was Gruyère. I despaired of the way they ruined tomatoes with vinaigrette. I could not understand why you had to eat all your meat before you got your vegetables. I wondered why they put grass-clippings in their omelettes. I loathed red wine. Nor was it just the alimentary apprehension: I was nervous about the language, the sleeping arrangements, the hotels. The absorbed tensions of a family holiday played on me. I was not happy, to put the matter simply. Like most adolescents, I needed the science of imaginary solutions. Is all nostalgia false, I wonder, and all sentimentality the representation of unfelt emotions?

Jean-Luc Cazes, I discovered from my encyclopaedia, was a writer invented by the OULIPO group and used as a front for various promotional and provocational enterprises. *Marrant* is the French for funny, which of course I had known before I set off: where else would you expect a pataphysical encounter to take place? I have not seen any of my fellow participants since that day, which isn't surprising. And I have still never been to a literary conference.

# DRAGONS

PIERRE CHAIGNE, carpenter, widower, was making a lantern. Standing with his back to the door of his workshed, he eased the four oblongs of glass into the runners he had cut and greased with mutton-fat. They moved smoothly and fitted well: the flame would be secure, and the lantern would cast its light in all directions, when this was required. But Pierre Chaigne, carpenter, widower, had also cut three pieces of beechwood the exact size of the panels of glass. When these were inserted, the flame would be cast in a single direction only, and the lantern would be invisible from three of the four compass points. Pierre Chaigne trimmed each piece of beechwood carefully, and when satisfied that they slid easily within the greased runners, he took them to a place of concealment among the discarded lumber at one end of the workshed.

Everything bad came from the north. Whatever else they believed, the whole town, both parts of it, knew that. It was the north wind, arching over the Montagne Noire, that made the ewes give birth to dead lambs; it was the north wind which put the devil into the widow Gibault and made her cry out, even at her age, for such things that she had to be stopped in the mouth with a cloth by her daughter, lest children or the priest hear what she wanted. It was to the north, in the forest on the other side of the Montagne Noire, that the Beast of Gruissan lived. Those who had seen it described a dog the size of a horse with the spots of a leopard, and many was the time, in the fields around Gruissan, that the Beast had taken livestock, even up to a small calf. Dogs sent by their masters to confront the Beast had had their heads bitten off. The town had petitioned the King, and the King sent his principal arquebusier. After much prayer and ceremony, this royal warrior had set off into the forest with a local woodsman, who shamefully had run away. The arquebusier emerged, several days later, empty-handed. He had returned to Paris, and the Beast had returned to its foraging. And now, they said, the dragons were coming, from the north, the north.

It was from the north, twenty years before, when Pierre Chaigne, carpenter, widower, had been a boy of thirteen, that the commissioners had come. They had arrived, the two of them, lace at the wrist and severity upon the face, escorted by ten soldiers. They examined the temple and heard evidence, from those who came forward, concerning the enlargements that had taken place. The next day, from a mounting-block, the senior of the commissioners had explained the law. The King's Edict, he said, had given protection to their religion, that was true; but such protection had been awarded only to the religion as it had been constituted at the time of the Edict. There had been no licence to enlarge their cult: the enemies of the King's religion had been granted toleration but not encouragement. Therefore all churches built by the religion since the Edict were to be torn down, and even those churches which had merely been enlarged were to be torn down as warning and instruction to those who continued to defy the King's religion. Further, to purge their crime, it was the builders of the temple themselves who were to demolish it.

Pierre Chaigne remembered at this point an outcry from those assembled. The Commissioner had thereupon announced that, in order to speed the work, four children from among the enemies of the King's religion had been placed under guard by the soldiers, and would be well and safely guarded, furnished with all that they required to eat, for as long as the dismantling of the temple might take. It was at this time that a great sadness came over the family of Pierre Chaigne, and shortly afterwards his mother had died of a winter fever.

And now the dragons were coming from the north. The priests of the King's religion had decreed that in the defence of the Holy Mother Church against the heretic anything was permissible, short of killing. The dragons themselves had another saying: What matter the road provided it led to Paradise? They had come, not so many years before, to Bougouin de Chavagne, where they had cast several of the menfolk into a great ditch at the base of the castle tower. The victims, broken by their fall, lost as in the darkness of the tomb, had comforted themselves by singing the 138th Psalm.

> *Though I walk in the midst of trouble, thou wilt revive me; thou shalt stretch forth thine hand against the wrath of mine enemies, and thy right hand shall save me.*

But as each night had passed, the voices from the great ditch had grown fewer, until the 138th Psalm was chanted no more.

The three soldiers placed into Pierre Chaigne's household were old men, forty years at least. Two of them had scars visible on their faces despite their great beards. On the shoulder of their leather tunics they wore the winged beast of their regiment. An additional whorl of stitching indicated to those with military knowledge that these old men belonged to the *dragons étrangers du roi*. Pierre Chaigne had no such understanding, but he had ears, and they were enough. These men did not seem to follow anything Pierre Chaigne said to them, and spoke among themselves the rough tongue of the north, the north.

They were accompanied by the Secretary of the Intendant, who read a short decree to Pierre Chaigne and his assembled family. It being given that the household of Pierre Chaigne, carpenter, widower, by its wilful failure to pay the tallage, was in odious breach of the King's law, the dragons, one officer and two men, would be quartered upon the Chaigne family, who were to supply such needs as they might have until such time as the household chose to pay the tallage and raise the burden from themselves. When the Secretary of the Intendant withdrew, one of the two common soldiers beckoned Pierre Chaigne's daughter Marthe towards him. As she advanced, he pulled from his pocket a small fighting animal which he held by the neck, and thrust it at her. Marthe, though merely thirteen years of age, had no fear of the beast; her calmness encouraged the family and surprised the soldier, who returned the creature to the long pocket stitched into the side of his trouser.

Pierre Chaigne had been accounted an enemy of the King's religion, and thereby an enemy of the King, but he did not admit to either condition. He was loyal to the King, and wished to live in peace with the King's religion; but this was not permitted. The Intendant knew that Pierre Chaigne could not pay the tallage imposed, or that if he did pay it, the tallage would immediately be increased. The soldiers had been placed into the household in order to collect the tallage; but their very presence, and the cost of entertaining them, diminished still further any chance of payment. This was known and established.

The Chaigne household consisted of five souls: Anne Rouget, widow, sister of Pierre Chaigne's mother, who had come to them when her husband, a two-plough labourer, had died; after burying her husband according to the rites of the King's religion, she had accepted the cult of her sister's family. She had now passed fifty years of age, and was consequently growing feeble of mind, but still able to cook and make the house with her great-niece Marthe. Pierre Chaigne had also two sons, Henri, aged fifteen, and Daniel, aged nine. It was for Daniel that Pierre Chaigne felt the greatest alarm. The law governing the age of conversion had been twice changed. When Pierre himself had been an infant, it was established law that a child was not permitted to leave the church of his parents until he be fourteen years old, that age being considered sufficient to confirm mental capacity. Then the age had been reduced to twelve. But the new law had lowered it still further, to a mere seven years of age. The purpose of this change was clear. A child such as Daniel, not yet having the fixity of mind which comes with adult years, might be lured from the cult by the colours and scents, the finery and display, the fairground trickery of the King's religion. It was known to have happened.

The three *dragons étrangers du roi* indicated their needs with incomprehensible speech and lucid gesture. They were to occupy the bed, and the Chaigne family were to sleep where they liked. They were to eat at the table, the Chaigne family were to wait upon them and eat whatever they left. The key to the house was surrendered to the officer, as also were the knives which Pierre and his elder son naturally carried to cut their food.

The first evening, as the three soldiers sat waiting for their soup, the officer roared at Marthe as she was placing the bowls before them. His voice was loud and strange. 'My stomach will think that my throat is cut,' he shouted. The other soldiers laughed. Marthe did not understand. The officer banged on his bowl with his spoon. Then Marthe understood, and brought his food swiftly.

The Secretary of the Intendant had stated that the dragons had lawfully been placed into the Chaigne household to collect the tallage; and on the second day the three soldiers did make some attempt to discover any money or valuable property that might have been hidden. They turned out cupboards, looked beneath the bed, rooted in Pierre Chaigne's woodstacks. They searched with a kind of dutiful anger, not expecting to find anything concealed, but wishing it to be known that they had done what was formally demanded of them. Previous campaigns had taught them that the households they were first invited to occupy were never those of the rich. When their services had initially been engaged, many years ago at the end of the War, it had seemed obvious to the authorities to quarter the dragons with those who were best able to pay the tallage. But this method proved slow; it strengthened the sense of fraternity among members of the cult, and produced some notable martyrs, the memory of whom often inspired the obstinate. Therefore it had been found more profitable to place the soldiers in the first instance into the families of the poor. This produced a useful division among the enemies of the King's religion, when the poor observed that the rich were exempt from the sufferings inflicted upon them. Swift conversions were many times thus obtained.

On the second evening, the soldier who kept the ferret

in his long knee-pocket pulled Daniel on to his knee as the boy offered him some bread. He grasped Daniel so firmly by the waist that the infant immediately began to struggle. The soldier held in his free hand a knife with which he intended to cut his bread. He put the blade flat against the table, which was made from the hardest wood known to Pierre Chaigne, carpenter, widower, and with only a gentle push raised a crisp, transparent curl from the surface of the table.

''Twould shave a mouse asleep,' he said. Pierre Chaigne and his family did not understand these words; nor did they need to.

On the next day the soldiers used the ferret to slaughter a cockerel, which they ate for dinner, and finding the house cold at midday, though the sun was shining, they broke up two chairs and burnt them in the chimney, ignoring the pile of firewood beside it.

Unlike the King's religion, the cult could be celebrated anywhere that the faithful gathered, without attendance at the temple. The dragons made efforts to prevent the family of Pierre Chaigne from fulfilling their observances: the house was locked at night, and the three soldiers disposed themselves during the day so that they could spy upon the movements of the family. But they were outnumbered by five to three, and it happened sometimes that escape was possible, and thereby a visit to a house where the cult was being celebrated. Pierre Chaigne and his family openly talked of such matters in front of the dragons; and it seemed a kind of sweet revenge to do so. But the dragons in the town, who numbered around forty, had sources of intelligence, and although the members of the cult frequently changed the house in which they met, they were as frequently discovered by the soldiers. So the enemies of the King's religion chose to gather in the open air, in the forest to the north of the town. At first they met by day, and later only by night. Many feared that the Beast of Gruissan would descend upon them in the darkness, and the first prayer offered up was always a plea to be defended from the Beast. One night they were surprised by the dragons, who ran at them screaming, then beat and cut them with their swords, chasing them from the forest. The next morning, when the widow Gibault was not to be found, they returned to the forest and discovered her there, dead of the shock.

Pierre Chaigne was able to remember a time when the two populations of the town moved freely among one another, when a funeral or a marriage was celebrated by the whole community, without regard for the creed of the participants. It was true that neither the adherents of the King's religion nor the members of the cult would enter one another's place of ritual; but one group would wait patiently outside for the ceremony to be completed, and then the whole town would follow, whether to the graveyard or to the wedding-feast. But shared rejoicing and shared grief had fallen equally into desuetude. Similarly, it was now rare in the town for a family to contain members of both faiths.

Though it was summer, the dragons were in need of fire. They burnt all the furniture except that which they needed for their own use. Then they began to burn the finest wood of Pierre Chaigne, carpenter, widower. Lengths of weathered oak from trees cut by his father twenty years ago, prime sections of elm and ash, all were consumed by fire. To increase Pierre Chaigne's indignity and misery, he was himself made to saw the timber into combustible lengths. When the dragons observed that this fine wood burnt more slowly than they had hoped, they ordered Pierre Chaigne and his sons to build a great bonfire beside the workshed, and instructed them to keep the fire alight until all Pierre Chaigne's wood was consumed.

As Pierre Chaigne stood looking at the mound of ashes which was all that remained of his future as a carpenter, the officer said to him, 'God's help is nearer than the door.' Pierre Chaigne did not understand these words.

Next the soldiers took all Pierre Chaigne's tools, and those of his son Henri, and sold them to members of the King's religion. At first Pierre Chaigne felt his misery lift, for having deprived him of his timber the soldiers did him no further harm depriving him of his tools; and besides, the sale of all his fine implements might even bring in money enough to pay the tallage and so make the soldiers depart. However, the dragons sold Pierre Chaigne's tools not for their value, but for a price so low that no one could resist buying them, and then kept the money for themselves. François Danjon, miller, widower, member of the King's religion, who had bought several of the instruments, returned them to Pierre Chaigne under cover of darkness. Pierre Chaigne wrapped them in oiled cloths and buried them in the woods against a better day.

It was at this time that a pedlar, aged nineteen, passing through the town on foot from the direction of the Cherveux, was seized by several dragons and interrogated. He had the suspicious accent of the south. After being beaten, he admitted to membership of the cult; after being beaten further, he admitted that he desired to abjure. He was taken before the priest, who gave him absolution and copied his name into the register of abjuration. The pedlar made a mark beside his name, and two of the dragons, proud of their zeal and trusting that it would be recompensed, signed as witnesses. The pedlar was sent on his way without his goods. Henri Chaigne, aged fifteen, watched the beating, which was done in the public square; and as the victim was taken off to the church, a dragon whom he had not before seen said to him in the coarse language of the north, 'What matter the road provided it lead to Paradise?' Henri Chaigne did not understand what was being said, but recognised the word Paradise.

At first conversions came quickly among the old, the feeble, the solitary, and those infants who had been forcibly beguiled by gaudy display. But after a few weeks the number of abjurations diminished. This was often the pattern, and it was known that the dragons frequently gave way to excesses in order that the conversions continue.

When the tallage had first been announced, there were those who had sought to flee, who had heard that it was possible to reach St Nazaire and discover the promised land elsewhere. Two families had left the town in this manner, whereupon members of the cult had been instructed by the Intendant to pull down and destroy with fire the houses they had left behind, whereupon the unpaid tallage was not forgotten but transferred to those who remained. It was always the way. When a heretic converted to the King's religion, his tallage was divided among the community of heretics, and their tax thus became even larger as their means of payment diminished. This led some to despair; but others, having lost everything, were made the more determined not to lose that faith on whose account they had already lost everything. Thus the booted missionaries met with more resistance as their work continued. This too was known and expected.

It was not long after Pierre Chaigne's instruments had

been sold that Anne Rouget, his mother's sister, fell into sickness and became the first member of the family to abjure. When the dragons saw that she was weak and feverish, they yielded the bed to her and slept upon the floor. This chivalry was deliberate, for no sooner was she positioned in the bed than the soldiers declared her sickening unto death and summoned the priest of the King's religion. It was established by royal ordinance that when a protestant heretic was dying, the priest had the right to visit the deathbed and offer the suffering one an opportunity to return in death to the Holy Mother Church. This visit, which the family were forbidden to prevent, was to take place in the presence of a magistrate; and the priest was not allowed to use any duress when attempting to obtain a conversion. However, such terms and conditions were not always strictly followed. The magistrate being occupied elsewhere, the priest was accompanied into the Chaigne household by the officer of the dragons. The family was expelled into the day's heat, two dragons guarded the door, and at the end of six hours Anne Rouget had been received back into the Church where she had spent the first thirty years of her life. The priest departed with satisfaction, and that night the soldiers reclaimed the bed as their own and returned Anne Rouget to the floor.

'Why?' asked Pierre Chaigne.

'Leave me in peace,' replied Anne Rouget.

'Why?'

'One or the other is true.'

She did not speak beyond that, and died two days later, though whether from her fever, her despair or her apostasy Pierre Chaigne was unable to determine.

The child Daniel, aged nine, was the next to abjure. He was taken to the church of the King's religion, where it was explained to him that Anne Rouget, who had done the service of a mother for him, was awaiting him in Heaven, and that he would surely see her again one day unless he clung to heresy and chose to burn in Hell. Then he was shown fine vestments and the gilt reliquary containing the little finger of Saint Boniface; he smelt the incense and examined the monsters carved between the choir-stalls – monsters which he would doubtless meet in person if he freely chose to burn in Hell. And the following Sunday, during the Mass, Daniel Chaigne publicly abjured the cult of the temple. His conversion was received with great and impressive solemnity, and afterwards he was much petted by the women of the King's religion. The following Sunday Pierre Chaigne and his elder son tried to prevent the dragons taking Daniel Chaigne to the Mass; they were beaten and the boy was taken none the less. He did not return, and Pierre Chaigne was informed by the priest that he had been placed beyond the reach of treason in the Jesuit College on the other side of the Montagne Noire, and that his education there would be at the expense of the family until such time as they chose to repudiate their heresy.

Only the obstinate ones now remained among the heretics. It was at this point that the Intendant named as Collector of the Tallage the leading Protestant landowner of the region, Pierre Allonneau, sieur de Beaulieu, fermier de Coutaud. It became his legal duty instantly to pay the accumulated tax owed by all members of the cult since the tallage was announced. This he was unable to do, but being reduced at once to ruin, was no longer able to help in secrecy the obstinate ones.

The three dragons had been within the Chaigne household for two months. All the chickens and both the pigs had been eaten; all but a little of the furniture had been burnt; Pierre Chaigne's timber had been consumed with the exception of a rough pile of worthless lumber at the back of his shed. Others in the town who might have supported the family were now equally destitute. Each day Pierre Chaigne and his son Henri were obliged to traverse the woods and fields to obtain food. Two of the soldiers came with them, leaving the officer to guard Marthe. It was difficult to find enough food to satisfy six mouths, and the two dragons offered no assistance in the chase of a rabbit or the search for mushrooms. When there was not enough food for the soldiers to eat until they belched, the Chaigne family went hungry.

It was on their return from one of these daily expeditions that Pierre Chaigne and Henri Chaigne discovered that the officer had taken Marthe Chaigne, aged thirteen, into the bed with him. This sight caused Pierre Chaigne much anger and despair; only his religion prevented him from seeking that very same night the death of the officer.

The following day the officer chose to accompany the two heretics on the search for food, and one of the ordinary soldiers stayed behind to guard Marthe. This soldier also took her into the bed with him. No explanation was offered, and none was required. Marthe Chaigne refused to talk to her father or her brother about what had been done.

After nine days of seeing his sister taken as a whore, Henri Chaigne abjured his faith. But this action did not prevent the dragons from continuing to take his sister as a whore. Consequently, at the celebration of Mass the following Sunday, Henri Chaigne spat out of his mouth the holy wafer and the holy wine he had received from the priest. For this blasphemy against the body and blood of Our Lord, Henri Chaigne was duly tried by the Bishop's court, condemned to death and handed over to the soldiers who burnt him with fire.

Afterwards, the three soldiers separated Pierre Chaigne and his daughter, not permitting them to talk to one another. Marthe kept the house and whored for the dragons; her father hunted for nourishment and cut wood in the forest, since the autumn air was now turning cold. Pierre Chaigne, who had suffered greatly, was resolved to resist apostasy even unto death. His daughter was equally certain in her faith, and underwent her daily ordeal with the fortitude of a martyr.

One morning, after the officer had taken her into the bed with him but treated her less roughly for once, she received a brutal surprise. The officer had been accustomed to talk to her in the rough language of the north while he used her as a whore, to shout words and afterwards to mutter quietly. She had become familiar with this, and at times it helped her bear the suffering more easily, for she was able to imagine that the man who spoke these words from the north was himself as distant as the north.

Now, as he still lay athwart her, he said, 'You are brave, young girl.'

It took her a moment to realise that he had spoken her own language. He raised himself on an elbow and shunted off her. 'I admire that,' he went on, still in her language, 'and so I want to spare you further suffering.'

'You speak our tongue.'

'Yes.'

'So you have understood what we have said in the house since you came here?'

'Yes.'

'And the others too?'

'We have been in your country many years.'

Marthe Chaigne was silent. She remembered what her brother Henri had openly said about the dragons, and about the priest of the King's religion. Her father had revealed where the cult was to be celebrated, little suspecting the consequences. She herself had uttered words of hatred.

'And because I wish to spare you suffering,' the officer continued, 'I shall explain what will happen.'

What could happen? More pain of this kind. Worse. Torture. Death. No doubt. But then Paradise, surely.

'What will happen is that you will become with child. And then we shall testify that your father used you as a whore in our presence. And you will be taken before the court, your father and you, and there condemned. You will be burnt to death, you and your father, as also will be the child of this incestuous union within you.'

The soldier paused, and allowed the rigid girl fully to understand what he had said. 'You will abjure. You will abjure, and thereby you will save your father's life.'

'My father would rather die.'

'Your father does not have the choice. Only you have the choice whether your father dies or not. So you will abjure.'

Marthe Chaigne lay motionless in the bed. The soldier got up, adjusted his clothing, and sat at the table waiting for her to agree. He was wise enough in his profession not to add unnecessary words.

Eventually the girl said, 'Where do you come from?'

The soldier laughed at the unexpectedness of the question. 'From the north.'

'Where? *Where?*'

'A country called Ireland.'

'Where is that?'

'Beyond the water. Near to England.'

'Where is that?'

'Beyond the water too. In the north.'

The girl in the bed remained with her head turned away from the soldier. 'And why do you come so far to persecute us?'

'You are heretics. Your heresy endangers the Holy Mother Church. All, everywhere, have a duty to defend Her.'

'Thirty pieces of silver.'

The officer appeared close to anger, but kept in mind the purpose of the day.

'If you have not heard of England then you have not heard of Cromwell.'

'Who is he?'

'He is dead now.'

'Is he your King? Did he recruit you? To come here and persecute us?'

'No. On the contrary.' The soldier began to remember things it did no good to remember, things which had fixed his life for ever, many years ago. Childhood, its sights, and its terrifying sounds. The harsh voices of England. 'Yes, I suppose he did. He recruited me, you could say.'

'Then I curse his name and all his family.'

The officer sighed. Where could he begin? There was so much to unravel, and he was an old man now, past forty. The child did not even know where England was. Where could he begin? 'Yes,' said the officer wearily. 'You curse his name. I curse his name too. We both curse his name. And on Sunday you will abjure.'

That Sunday, while incense stung her nostrils and her eye was assailed by the whorish colours of the King's religion, Marthe Chaigne, aged thirteen, her heart burdened by the sorrow she was causing her father and by the knowledge that she would never be permitted to explain, abjured her faith. She made a mark on the register beside her name, and the officer of the dragons signed as witness. After he had signed, he looked up at the priest and said, in his own language, 'What matter the road provided it lead to Paradise?'

Marthe Chaigne was taken that day to the Union Chrétienne on the other side of the Montagne Noire, where she would be educated by the good sisters. The cost of her education would be added to the tallage owed by Pierre Chaigne.

The following week the dragons left the town. The heretics had been reduced in number from one hundred and seventy-six to eight. There were always the obstinate ones, but experience had shown that when they were greatly outnumbered they had little influence and ended their lives in bitterness and despair. The dragons were to move south and start their work in a new place.

The eight obstinate ones were burdened by the tallage of those who had converted, with the cost of educating their own children as Catholics, and with numerous additional imposts. By ordinance they were forbidden from practising their trade or from hiring out their labour to members of the King's religion. They were also forbidden from abandoning their homes and seeking the promised land elsewhere.

Two nights after the dragons left, Pierre Chaigne, carpenter, widower, returned to his workshed. He took down the lantern he had made and slid out three of its glass panels. From the pile of discarded lumber too contemptible even to be burnt by the soldiers he uncovered the three oblongs of thin beechwood. He pushed them gently between the runners sticky with mutton-fat. Then he lit the candle and set the hood back in place. Lacking three-quarters of its glass, the instrument did not illuminate universally. But it gave a brighter, purer light for the direction in which it was pointed. Pierre Chaigne, carpenter, widower, would follow that light to the end of its journey. He walked to the door of his shed, lifted the latch, and set off into the cold night. The yellow beam of his lamp reached tremblingly towards the forest, where the other obstinate ones waited for him to join them in prayer.

———————————————— o ————————————————

TELL YOU HOW I learned to descend. Mr Douglas, back then, kept telling me I rode like a postman. He had this old machine as well as his racer, stand-up handlebars, almost a shopping-basket on the front, and sometimes he'd go out on it with me. I thought he was just doing it to put me down, but he was a canny fellow, he was showing me how far I had to go. I mean, he wouldn't keep up with me all day, but he'd do it for a stretch, then send me off over the hills by myself. Uphill, downhill, story of my life.

So one day I thought training was over and he started towing me up Mount Moran. Just kept pedalling, mouth shut, setting the pace, with me in behind. We'd been out seven, eight hours already and the sun was turning all orange over the flats and I really didn't see the point because he wasn't hurting me, I was sitting on his back wheel and no problem. We'd gone up this whole load of big loops and he stops at the side of the road and we're looking into the sun and he says, 'Right, Andy, I'm going to teach you how to descend.' And – this is the scary bit – he takes out this little spanner and unscrews his brake blocks and just hands them to me. 'All you have to do is keep up,' he says, 'and I'll buy the drinks.' So he pushes off while I'm stowing his blocks, and I had to follow him, and at first I thought well if he isn't using brakes I won't either, except by the second or third bend I was cramming them on and here's this little old geezer, this flying fucking postman, speeding down ahead of me, just using his body to slow himself down, sitting up in the saddle and then going into a crouch and using every inch of the road and sometimes I'd do a bend like him without the brakes and I'd let out a yell but he'd have his mouth shut all the way, Mr Douglas.

Once or twice I caught up with him but I always lost it on the bends and *I* was shit-scared to think about having this old Raleigh and no brakes. And at the same time I could see that if you could do it, if you could really do it, it would be like having a jump or whatever. The most exciting thing there was. And each time we went up Mount Moran he'd do the same, except he'd say I could use the brakes six times, and then five, and then four, and then in the end no brakes at all. And I'd follow that lovely old bastard on his granny bike and he'd always beat me but less and less each time. Then I'd buy the drinks, and he'd tell me how to live my life. One day he told me about Brambilla. And that's how I learned to descend.

———————— o ————————

I ran away from home. No, the truth is, I was gone already, in my head, anyway. Of course they blamed Andy but that's ridiculous. Andy was the first boy who always brought me home sharp at eight-thirty. He said from the beginning he had to be in bed by nine because nine was when Sean Kelly went to bed. You'd think they'd approve of that but they didn't. My dad thought there was something wrong about it. I said Dad it makes a change from you waiting up after midnight with a shotgun. But he didn't think that was funny. He didn't get the point.

Yes, I suppose I did run away with Andy in their eyes. One day he said I'm off to pedal my way round France for a living, want to come? I said what? He said, take the brakes off and just go *whoosh*. I said, *whoosh?* And he winked, and that was it. But I was never staying. It's not Andy's fault I don't live down the street with two kids, backache and afternoons in a shop if I'm lucky. They couldn't understand why I didn't want to listen to the seagulls over the bowling-green for the rest of my life. If they wanted that for me, they shouldn't have let me go to ballet. Home sweet home. My dad even suggested I should try bowls, the club could do with some new blood. I said, you mean like Dracula? They kept asking what Andy and I had in common. I said, well, legs for a start.

We sat on the boat and looked out of the big back window. There was the usual flock of gulls but I somehow got the idea they were the ones from the bowling-green. I kept expecting them to turn back, but they didn't. There were probably other reasons as well but I started crying. Poor Andy didn't know what was happening. I said, they should have had enough by now. When he saw I was serious he went out on to the deck and I could see him swearing at the gulls and waving his fists. Of course they didn't take any notice, but it was very sweet. I dried my tears and gave him a kiss. I said something like, Who's my hero, and he said something like, I'm a hard man, doll. He's putting it on when he talks like that. Mostly. Then we both tried to ignore the fact that the gulls stayed with us, all the way to Calais. Never turned back.

———————  o  ———————

They respect us, you know. The anglophones, they call us. They know we're hard men, we haven't come all this way to throw in the towel. They still remember Tom Simpson as if it was yesterday. Did you know when he died on the Ventoux it was the thirteenth day of the month and the thirteenth stage of the race? Makes you think, doesn't it? He's still a hero out here, the one who paid the ultimate price. Next day, they let Barry Hoban take the stage as a mark of respect. An Englishman winning on the *quatorze juillet*. Barry Hoban married Tom Simpson's widow, did you know that?

Sean Kelly, he's the iron man. He eats nails for breakfast. Did you hear about Sean Kelly in the Tour of Spain? He had . . . there's a medical name for it but I've forgotten, but basically it's a sort of ingrowing hair in your arse. They used to get it in the war, called it Jeep Arse, you got it from riding round on the hard seat of a jeep all day. It's the most painful thing there is, and it's only, you know, one of the hairs in your arse deciding to grow in rather than out. That's all it is, but you get this boil which hurts like hell, and the worst thing you can do if you've got it is ride a bike. You have to get it surgically treated and then you're sitting in a salt bath for a few weeks. Anyway, Sean Kelly's in this good position in the Tour of Spain, so naturally he doesn't want any hassle. If he goes to the tour doctor he'll be ordered out of the race. So he gets this local surgeon or doctor or maybe vet to come to his hotel room and says Go ahead, do it. And the guy does it, and stitches his arse up and Sean Kelly carries on with the Tour of Spain. That's why they respect us. We're tough. Sean Kelly, he's the iron man.

---

We were having a meal with Betty and Jean-Luc. Betty's from Falmouth – she was on the cruise-ship with me. In fact, she got me the job out here; the audition anyway. It was our day off and we'd gone out to dinner. We always eat early because of Andy. I don't call it dinner any more, I call it *steak and a salad at seven says Sean*. Not that I'm allowed to call him Sean. Andy always says the name in full, as if it was a saint's name or something. It's Sean Kelly this and Sean Kelly that and I do the same. Mostly. So Andy was talking about how riders prepare for a race, and he told a story about a press conference where someone asked Sean Kelly about what he did about . . . you-know-what. I mean, obviously they don't do it during a race, but do they stop beforehand to conserve their energy. If I'd been Sean Kelly I'd have been tempted to wrap a bicycle pump round the fellow's head, but he didn't. He just answered the question. He said his policy was to abstain for a week before a big one-day race, and for six weeks before a major tour. Whereupon one fellow in the audience said in a loud voice, 'By my reckoning that makes Linda still a virgin.' Linda is Sean Kelly's wife. Wouldn't you have just died? Betty and Jean-Luc were looking at me as if to say, Is it like that for you too? I didn't know where to put myself. Most men I've been with would have been boasting about doing it more than we did. But here was Andy doing almost the opposite. I tried to explain afterwards but he said I was oversensitive. He just thought it was a funny story.

———————  o  ———————

I'm scared I won't get home. These first six days I've been working my arse off. I'm in the best condition of my life, and I've never been so tired. Yesterday we saw the Pyrenees in the distance. I can't think about them, I won't think about them. Each day it's five, six, seven hours in the saddle, then eat, then fall asleep, then team meeting then another seven, eight, nine hours in the saddle. In this heat. And after the Pyrenees, the Alps. I'll have to see the soigneur to get up some of those hills, I know that. He'll give me something. He'd better.

It's not like when I was starting. Then everyone had his little briefcase, like going to the office. Full of goodies. Tried this? Had this one? Here's something you need to take a bit earlier, and so on. Everyone needing a *whoosh* at the same time. You only get about three hours on amphets, so you'd need to take them before the big hills started. It was a good giggle, everyone taking them at the same time, then all these bits of silver paper thrown away like milk-bottle tops or something, and all at once you could feel the pace pick up, and everyone was laughing and hollering and *whoosh* we all went up the hill. It's not like that now. Not so many laughs. It's get me some water, take this message, give me your wheel, lead me out now. I thought the first few days would be easy, they might even let me go to the front if I felt good. But I've felt knackered since the Prologue, that's the truth.

We're pedalling across this flat plain for bloody hours, just staring at them. I've never seen mountains that high. I'm scared. It's downhill then uphill, isn't it? That's the truth, that's how it goes. Downhill, then uphill. I'm scared I won't get home.

———————— o ————————

I don't usually get back from the club till three, so by the time I'm awake he's already in the saddle. It's so frustrating,

I turn on the television but most of the jerseys look alike to me and in six days I don't think I've had a sight of him. Sometimes I'm almost sure I've spotted him and then the television cuts to a helicopter-shot and all you see is this great big snake of riders going through a village. And by the time his day's over, mine's already started. Andy is not the world's greatest postcard-writer either. I buy *L'Equipe* every day and read where he's been and what's ahead and run my finger down the classification lists for his name. He's 152nd at the moment out of 178.

Andy's inclined to bang on about how tough riding a bike is. I tell him I'm probably as fit as he is. Betty and I do six nights out of seven, thirteen shows a week. He has *steak and a salad at seven says Sean* and is in bed by nine, so by the time he's tucked up I've got two shows to do. Andy says riding a bike is all about character, as if other things weren't as well. Monsieur Thalabert says he never chooses any girl without a personality and it's true. We're all personalities in our different ways. When I want to needle Andy, I tell him anyone can ride a bike. Meaning you don't have to be a perfect 34 up top and the rest in proportion. You don't have to be five foot seven to the nearest centimetre. Neither do you have a rule saying you can't change your appearance in any way without the management's permission.

There are a lot of rules, but they're for our own protection. You aren't allowed to drink on the premises, you aren't allowed to meet any men within two hundred metres of the club, you have to stay the same weight, you have to turn up on time, you get your holidays when they tell you, and so on. That's why they like English girls. We've got good discipline as well as being the right shape. Of course, anyone caught with drugs gets sent straight home.

Sometimes I think it's strange when I look back. The girls are all very supportive, it's like one big family, and I think of the club as my home. But I ran away from home because my mum took my wages and gave me pocket-money while my dad laid down all these rules about how late I could stay out, how short my skirt could be and what sort of boys I could meet when and where. Now Monsieur Thalabert puts our money into a savings scheme and protects us from the wrong sort of men, while Madame Yvonne fusses all over us like a mother hen. Chreesteen, not that skirt. Chreesteen, be careful of that boy. And so on. But I don't mind a bit. I suppose it's the difference between the home you grow up in and the home you choose.

Some people wonder how you can take your clothes off in public. Well, I'm not ashamed of what nature's given me. And it's not exactly taking your clothes off when they're mostly off to begin with. As Betty puts it, everything's always covered with something, even if it's only nail-varnish. Everything's covered with something. You probably see as much of Andy when he's on his bike as you do of me when I'm on stage. My nan came over without telling Mum and Dad. She really enjoyed the show. She said it was tasteful, and she was proud of me.

———————— ○ ————————

This rider, it was a few years ago, he was going to be tested that day. It's meant to be random but, well, it wasn't like it is now, come in here and stick your prodder in a test-tube while a man in a white coat watches you do it. You could sometimes find out before, that morning anyway, and so you knew you'd have to be a bit more careful what sweeties you took. Anyway, this rider knows he's going to be tested at the end of the day and he's shitting himself. He's been overdoing it a bit lately, fellow with the briefcase been calling round a lot. So this is what he does. He tells his girlfriend to wait beside the road at a certain point, somewhere in the woods where there aren't too many people around. And then, as the peloton arrives, he says he's dropping back, stopping for a piss or something, maybe he said he'd spotted his girl and was going to give her a kiss. Anyway, he stops, and he's asked her to have a sample ready for him, you know, one of hers, in a placcy bag or something, so she does, and he gives her a kiss and slips it down his jersey. So at the end of the day they tell him to give a sample, and he takes the tube and goes into the toilet and comes back and hands it over, easy as pie. Next morning he's called back by the doctors and he's really surprised because he knows he must have tested clean. He can't think what to expect. And you know what they say to him? 'François,' or whatever his name is, 'François, the good news is you're clean. The bad news is you're pregnant.'

---

Another of Andy's stories is about Linda and Sean Kelly waiting for Stephen Roche to take a dope test. This was during the 1984 Amstel Gold Classic. In Meersten. That's in Holland. You see, I know all the details by now. So while they were waiting, Linda was sitting on their car, and when she got up she left a mark where her hand had been. Sean Kelly, according to Andy, is a very particular man. He took a handkerchief out of his pocket and wiped away the mark. Didn't say a word, just wiped away the mark. Linda said something to him like, I can see what your priorities are, first the car, then the bike and then the wife. Sean Kelly looks at her, completely serious, and do you know what he says? He says, 'The bike comes first.'

We get on well enough. The worst row we had was early on. I'd been looking in the French papers for his name and when I found it I saw they called him *un domestique*. That's French for a servant. And since he'd been coming on a bit macho about how the French really respected British riders because they were so tough, I said, so you're just a servant then? He said it was only his second year on the team so of course he had to fetch other people's water-bottles and pass messages and give up a wheel or sometimes his whole bike if someone more important needed it, for instance if they had a puncture. He said he was part of a team, one for all and all for one. I thought he was being a bit pompous, so instead of biting my tongue I said it sounded more like all for one and not much one for all. He said what the eff did I know, except that I should because I was just the same when I danced, one of a team, and I shouldn't make the mistake of thinking anyone had come to see me. I remember exactly what he said next. He said I was just a tiny bit of topping on a pizza and I should remember that next time I was waggling my fanny, only he didn't say fanny. And how we were two of a kind. Only he didn't say it nicely, as if we were well matched, two against the world, like it had been when we started out. It was more as if I wasn't much better than a mess on the pavement and he wasn't much better either. Everything just went wrong in seconds. Do you know that feeling? It always makes me think of the seagulls. They never turned round and went back. He waved his arms at them and swore but they took no notice. They followed us here, all the way.

You can imagine how miserable I felt. He was still angry but after a bit we went to bed and . . . well, he didn't have a bike race in the immediate future. Except that it never quite works, like that, does it? There's always a bit of you thinking, I know why we're doing it, and is it the same for you. Afterwards he said, you never know when you're going to lose your back wheel, do you? You just feel it slide and then you wait for the road to rip the skin from your body. He didn't just mean me. He meant everything.

———————  o  ———————

When Sean Kelly and Linda got married, guess what his mates did? You know how, outside the church, if it's a soldier or something gets married, they all hold their swords over their heads as the couple comes out? Well Sean Kelly's mates held up a couple of racing-bikes to make an arch, then he and Linda walked out beneath it. Don't you like that?

The priest who married them gave this speech, he said marriage was like the Tour de France, how it went over different sorts of terrain, and different roads, and how sometimes the going was easy and sometimes it was difficult, and so on and all that sort of thing. And Sean Kelly gets up and this is what he says. 'One thing about Father Butler's speech. I don't think marriage and the Tour de France are exactly the same. If things are going bad in a bike race, you can simply climb off.'

Except that's not easy either. We get a rest day before the Pyrenees. I don't know if that's better or worse. Everyone's scared of the high mountains. You know what the riders say about the mountains: they strip you and leave you naked, that's what they say. The climbing, the thin air, the crazy descents. Those birds in the air, hovering. Big birds, the sort that eat rabbits and stuff. You just have to remember everyone else is scared. And you never get used to it, that's what they say. Have you heard of Alpe d'Huez? That's in the Alps. There was one top rider who was shit-scared of it, so one year he took his training partner and went there for his holidays. They climbed it twenty times until he lost his fear of it. Twenty times. Next year, when the Tour came to Alpe d'Huez, he wasn't frightened. That was a mistake. The mountain blew him away.

The broom-wagon, that's what it's called, that's the worst thing. It sweeps you up. Follows behind with a broom-stick attached to its roof, just waiting for you to fail. It's there all the time, haunting the last man on the road. I had it alongside me today. Want to come in, want to get home, that's a nasty fall you had, muscles must be aching by now, nice soft seat inside. Sweep, sweep. It's like some bloody tempter coming alongside. Won't have to worry any more, won't have to pedal. Put your feet up. Take the short-cut to home. No one gets round Le Grand Boucle the first time, you've done more than everyone expected. Don't wreck yourself for the rest of the season. Come on, get inside. Sweep, sweep, keep the road nice and tidy. Can't exactly fetch water for your team leader when you're twenty-five minutes behind, can you? Don't give me that shit about pride. No one's blaming you. Come inside, put your feet up, there's plenty of room for more. Sweep, sweep. Look at those mountains. They strip you, and they leave you naked.

———————  o  ———————

Very early on Andy told me another story. He was trying to impress me about how *hard* everyone was. I've come to hate that word, you know. So Saint Sean Kelly had something wrong with his bottom. I don't remember the details, except that of course it was more painful than anything a woman could possibly understand. He had some treatment and it went on being just as painful but he carried on riding anyway. It wasn't in France, for some reason I remember that. Anyway, when Andy had finished telling the story I could see I was meant to be impressed but it sounded . . . not exactly stupid, but let's say I wasn't open-mouthed. So I said, what happened? Andy said, what do you mean, what happened? I said, so Sean Kelly won the race? Andy said no, and I said, well it wasn't worth it then, was it? And I could see he was getting cross. He said all right I'll tell you what happened seeing as how you're so interested. What happened was he went on with the race, and a day or two later his stitches burst when he was in the saddle and his shorts were full of blood and he had to retire, now do you see why I admire him? Well I said yes, but I'm not sure I didn't mean no.

———————— ○ ————————

Mr Douglas told me about Brambilla. The name won't mean anything to you unless you're one of us. He was an Italian. Way back then. Lost the Tour on the very last day, which isn't something that happens often. That's not why Mr Douglas told me about him. He was a real pro. A hard man. When he thought he was riding badly he used to slap himself round the face and whack himself with his pump and not let himself have any water even though he had some left. Tough character. You have to be a bit crazy as well to do what we do. Anyway, he was a well-known rider, and he'd had a good career, and he was getting a bit long in the tooth. And one day his mates went to see him, and they found him at the bottom of his garden. He'd been digging this sort of pit, well more a narrow trench but really deep. And you know what he was doing? He was burying his bicycle. Burying it upright, like it was when he rode it. And his mates asked him what he was up to. And Brambilla told them what he was doing. He was burying his bicycle because in his opinion he was no longer worthy to ride it. Mr Douglas said I should never forget this story, and I haven't.

THEY SAW IT FROM the Pauillac steamer, its pocked façade still quarter-lit by the early afternoon sun. They had embarked at Bordeaux, near the Place des Quinconces, at eleven, taking their place in cane seats beneath a striped awning. On the foredeck immediately below them clustered the third-class passengers, equipped with livestock, energy and noise. Florence felt debilitated by the evidence of normal vivacity undiscouraged by the heat; yet Emily seemed to feed from it.

'Look at that man, Florence. He does not just talk. He . . . he *dances* his conversation.'

'I expect he is saying something very mundane.'

'If so,' Emily came back, undaunted, 'if so, then his manner permits him to transcend the mundane.' She took out her sketch-book and began to draw the capering, sharp-nosed fellow, with his bare head, blue blouse, stubby pipe and liquid hands.

'I wish I discovered as much transcending as you, my dear Emily. It seems all around you. Now you transcend the man some more by turning him into art.'

'You shan't put me out of humour. And besides, we all believe in transcendence. You merely disguise it by calling it practical improvement.'

They sat quietly, two Englishwomen in their thirties, sailor-hats and brown shoes apiece, while the steamer headed past a winter woodland of ships' masts. Steam whistles were the loudest birdsong here. A tugboat named *Ercule* churned froth on the *café au lait* river; lesser ferries scudded across their bows like water-spiders. They had been away three weeks, and were at the most southerly point of their journey. Soon, as every year, they would be heading back to their separate Essex villages, to winds from the Urals and the chill conversation of turnip-farmers. Of course, these dinner clods cultivated other crops, but this was how, in their private conversations, Florence and Emily invariably designated them.

'I shall never marry,' said Florence suddenly. She made it sound a matter of fact but not regret.

'In any case,' her friend replied, continuing, or perhaps duplicating, the thought, 'it is well known that a turnip-farmer is beyond any possible transcendence.'

The little steamer tacked from bank to bank, picking up and depositing merchants and peasants, livestock and priests. The Garonne embraced the Dordogne and became the Gironde. Emily's skirt bulged with the wind until she pressed down on it a map marked with the châteaux of the Médoc. She settled a small pair of field-glasses over her spectacles and adopted a scholarly hunch familiar to her fellow-traveller. Alongside Beychevelle, Emily explained that the château had once belonged to an admiral, that every ship passing along the river had been at one time obliged to lower its sail, or *baisser la voile*, in homage, and that this phrase had been corrupted into the present name.

'Quite fanciful,' commented Florence cheerfully.

Emily indicated Margaux and Ducru-Beaucaillou, Léoville-las-Cases and Latour, appending Baedeker embellishments to each name. Beyond Latour, the boat ran close to the bank as it headed up towards Pauillac. Ribbed vineyards ran away from them like green corduroy. A broken-down pier came into sight, followed by a patch of corduroy stained half-black. Then, a little higher up, a flat façade made biscuity by the sun, with a brief terrace half-obscuring the ground-floor windows. After a nudge of focusing, Emily detected that several balusters were missing from the balcony of the terrace, and others badly askew. Florence took the glasses. The façade had large holes gouged into it, there were some broken upper window-panes, while the roof appeared to have been given over to experimental agriculture.

'Not exactly our hermitage,' she commented.

'So we shall visit tomorrow?'

This teasing pastime had evolved during the last two years of their French excursions. Idling glances proposed a different life: in a timbered Normandy farmhouse, a trim Burgundy *manoir*, a backwater château of the Berry. Lately, a new gravity of intention had arisen, which neither woman could quite admit. So Florence would announce that their hermitage had again not been found, and soon afterwards they would visit.

Château Dauprat-Bages had not been listed in the great Classification of 1855. It was a modest *cru bourgeois*, 16 hectares planted with cabernet sauvignon, merlot and petit verdot. During the last decade phylloxera had blackened its green corduroy, and some hesitant replanting had begun under its enfeebled and impoverished owner. Three years previously he had died, leaving all to a young nephew in Paris, who snobbishly preferred Burgundy and sought to divest himself of Château Dauprat-Bages as quickly as possible. But no neighbouring estate could be persuaded to take on the blighted vineyards; the *régisseur* and the *homme d'affaires* had therefore struggled on with casual labour, producing a wine which even they admitted had sunk to the level of a *cru artisan*.

When Florence and Emily returned for their second visit, Monsieur Lambert, the *homme d'affaires*, a short, black-suited man with a felt cap and a spiky moustache, his manner both fussy and domineering, turned suddenly to Emily, whom he judged the younger, and therefore the more dangerous of the two, and demanded, 'Êtes-vous Américaniste?'

Misunderstanding him, she replied, 'Anglaise.'

'Américaniste?' he reiterated.

'Non,' she replied, and he grunted approval. She felt she had passed some test without having been told what the test might be.

Next morning, over a breakfast of oysters and hot sausages at the Hôtel d'Angleterre in Pauillac, Florence said musingly, 'You cannot say that they have landscape here. It is more that they have contours.'

'Then it will not seem entirely a change from Essex.'

Both observed the seduction of *might* and *could* into *is* and *will*. They had travelled in France together for five summers now. In hotels they shared the same bed; at meals they permitted themselves wine; after dinner Florence would smoke a single cigarette. Each year had been a heady escape, both a justification of their life among the turnip-farmers and a rebuke to it. Their excursions among the French had so far been light-hearted, flirtatious. Emily now felt as if something – not destiny, but the lesser organisation that directed their lives – was calling her bluff.

'However, it is your money,' she said, acknowledging that things had become very serious indeed.

'It was my father's money and I shall have no children.'

Florence, the larger and slightly older of the two, had an

oblique way of announcing decisions. She was dark and sturdy, with a deceptive style of down-to-earth discouragement. In truth, she was both more capable and more benign than she appeared, despite a docile preference for only the broader aspects of any project. Emily could always be relied upon to take care of the particularities; Emily, slim, blonde, neatly fussy, peering through gold-wired spectacles at notebook, sketch-pad, timetable, newspaper, menu, Baedeker, map, ticket and legal fine print; Emily, fretful yet optimistic, who now said wonderingly, 'But we know nothing of making wine.'

'We are not applying for posts as vendangeuses,' Florence replied, with a lazy hauteur that was not wholly self-mocking. 'Father did not understand how the saw-mill operated, but he knew that gentlemen required desks. Besides, I am sure that you will study the matter. It cannot be more complicated than . . . cathedrals.' She threw this out as a recent example, since in her view they had spent excessive time beneath the statue of Bertrand de Goth, Archbishop of Bordeaux and later Pope Clement V, while Emily expounded on 12th-century Romanesque arches in the nave and a choir with double stalls from some other – no doubt earlier, or later – century.

The Burgundian nephew accepted Florence's offer, and she sold her house in Essex; Emily informed brother Lionel, the solicitor, that he would have to find himself another housekeeper (news she had longed to impart for some years). In the spring of 1890 the two women transplanted themselves irrevocably to France, taking with them no specific reminders of England except the grandfather-clock which had marked every hour of Florence's childhood. As their train pulled away from the quai d'Austerlitz at the Gare d'Orléans, Emily yielded up a final anxiety.

'You shall not be bored? I mean, with my company. This is not just an excursion.'

'I have decided the château will bear your name,' Florence replied. 'I have always thought Dauprat-Bages quite lacking in romance.' She re-pinned her hat, as if to ward off any protest. 'In the matter of the turnip-farmers, I do not think their memory will fade so quickly. Such dancers! The clods scarcely noticed when they trod upon one!'

Mme Florence and Mme Emily re-engaged M. Lambert as *homme d'affaires* and M. Collet as *régisseur* on improved terms. M. Lambert then found them a housekeeper, three estate workers, a maid and a gardener. The shrubbery was dug out of the roof, the balusters mended, the pock-marked façade filled in, the pier rebuilt. Florence occupied herself with the house and presided over the newly-planted *potager;* Emily directed relations with the vineyard. The commune of Dauprat welcomed the women: they brought employment, and wished to restore a damaged vineyard to prosperity. No one objected when Château Dauprat-Bages became Château Haut Railly. *Les Anglaises* may have lacked religion, but they entertained the curé to tea each November, and solemnly attended his annual benediction of the vines in April. Such eccentricities as were observed could be lightly ascribed to the impoverished existence they must have previously endured on that distant island in whose cold, wet climate not even an Alsatian vine could flourish. It was noted, for instance, that they were great enthusiasts for domestic economy. A roast fowl might last them a week; soap and string were used until their final centimetre; linen was spared by the women's sharing a bed.

In late September a band of genial ruffians descended for the *vendange;* they were awarded huge dinners, and allowed to drink as much of the previous year's *petit vin* as they wished.

Florence and Emily were impressed that drunkenness did not ensue. They were also surprised to see men and women working harmoniously alongside one another in the vineyard. M. Lambert explained that the women were paid less on the grounds that they talked more. With a few sly shakes of the head, he then described a particular local tradition. It was strictly forbidden for any of the *vendangeurs* to eat the grapes they were picking, and at the end of each morning the women were obliged to put out their tongues for inspection. If the proof was purple, then the overseer would be entitled to claim a kiss in punishment. Florence and Emily kept to themselves the reflection that this sounded a little primitive, while the *homme d'affaires* concluded, with a wink bordering on impertinence, 'Of course, sometimes they eat deliberately.'

When the first vintage was safely gathered in, the *bal des vendangeurs* ensued. Trestle tables were laid out in the courtyard, and on this occasion the effects of alcohol were more readily apparent. Two fiddlers and a squeezebox goaded the heavy-kneed vintagers into some dancing which, even so, displayed a grace and energy way beyond those of the most teetotal turnip-farmer. There being insufficient women present, Florence enquired of M. Lambert as to the propriety of his partnering the château's new owner. The *homme d'affaires* pronounced the suggestion an honour, but felt, if he was being invited to offer guidance to Madame, that others in the same situation would choose to watch from the head of the table. Florence therefore tapped her foot in irritated resignation as slight and wiry Frenchmen slung around women who for the most part were taller, plumper and older. After an hour or so, M. Lambert clapped his hands, and the youngest *vendangeuse* shyly brought Florence and Emily each a bunch of heliotropes. Emily delivered a short speech of thanks and congratulations, whereupon the two women retired to bed, listening through their open window to the whirl and stamp from the courtyard, to the scratch of the fiddles and the indefatigable jauntiness of the squeezebox.

Emily became, to Florence's indulgent dismay, even more learned in viticulture than in church architecture. The matter was the more confusing since Emily rarely knew the correct English word for the terms she was employing. Sitting in a cane chair on the terrace with the sun glistening the loose hair at the nape of her neck, she would lecture Florence on the parasitical enemies and cryptogamic maladies of the vine. *Altise*, Florence heard, and *rhynchite; cochinelle, grisette, érinose;* there were monstrous beasts called *l'ephippigère de Béziers* and *le vespère de Xatart;* then there was *le mildiou* and *le black-rot* (those at least she understood), *l'anthracnose* and *le rot blanc*. Emily saw these disasters in coloured illustration as she spoke: shredded leaves, noxious spottings and wounded branches filled her spectacles. Florence tried to show the proper concern.

'What is a cryptogamic malady?' she asked dutifully.

'Cryptogamia, according to Linnaeus, comprise those plants which have no stamens or pistils, and therefore no flowers, such as mosses, algae, funghi. Mosses and lichens too. From the Greek, meaning concealed wedlock.'

'Cryptogamia,' Florence repeated like a pupil.

'It is Linnaeus's last class of plants,' Emily added. She was now at the extremity of her knowledge, but pleased that Florence seemed for once to be following her there.

'Last, but I am sure not least.'

'I do not know if the categories imply moral judgment.'

'Oh, I am sure not,' Florence asserted firmly, though she was no botanist. 'But how sad that some of our enemies are cryptogamic,' she added.

Emily's discussion of these selfsame maladies with M. Lambert was more complete but less satisfactory. It seemed evident to her that the researches of L'École Nationale d'Agriculture at Montpellier were convincing, and that the ravages of phylloxera should be repaired with vines grafted upon American rootstocks. Professor Millardet of Bordeaux agreed, even if there had been lively differences of opinion in the viticultural press.

To M. Lambert the matter was not at all so evident; indeed, quite the contrary. He reminded Mme Emily, who was a recent arrival in the Médoc, that the European vine, for all its many variations, consisted of but a single species, *vinis vitifera*, whereas the American vine comprised nearly two dozen different species. The European vine had existed in a state of almost perfect health for more than two millennia, and the maladies now afflicting it were entirely due, as had been proved beyond the least doubt, to the introduction of the American vines into France. Thus, he continued – and at this juncture Emily began to suspect that they had read the same volume – thus, there had been the appearance of oïdium in 1845, of phylloxera in 1867, of mildew in 1879, and of black-rot in 1884. Whatever professors in universities might believe, his colleagues in the vineyards had the opinion that you did not, when confronted by a disease, cure it by importing its cause. To put matters as plainly as possible, if you had a child with pneumonia, you did not seek to cure it by putting into its bed another child already suffering from influenza.

When Emily pressed the argument for grafting, M. Lambert's face tightened, and he banged his felt cap against his thigh. 'Vous avez dit que vous n'étiez pas Américaniste,' he said plainly, as if forcing an end to the discussion.

Only now, with her studies behind her, did Emily

appreciate the question she had been asked on their second tour of inspection. The world here divided into *sulfureurs* and *Américanistes:* those for whom salvation from phylloxera lay in rescuing and restoring pure French vines by chemical treatment, and those who wished to turn the vineyards into some new California. Her earlier reply to M. Lambert had unwittingly confirmed to him that she was a *sulfureur*, or rather, as he now put it, with what might have been either linguistic correctness or light sarcasm, a *sulfureuse*. If she was now telling him that she had changed her mind and was an *Américaniste* after all, then he and M. Collet, grateful though they were to Mme Florence and Mme Emily, would feel, to say the least, deceived.

'Who are we to say?' was Florence's response when Emily explained the dilemma.

'Well, we – you – are the owner. And I have been reading the very latest viticultural press.'

'My father never knew how the saw-mill worked.'

'Even so, the legs of his desks did not, I trust, fall off.'

'Dear Emily,' said Florence, 'you do worry so.' She smiled, then gave an indulgent chuckle. 'And I shall think of you from now on as my *sulfureuse*. Yellow has always suited you.' She chuckled again. The matter, Emily realised, had been both avoided and concluded by Florence: such was often her way.

What Florence called 'worrying' was to Emily a proper concern for husbandry. She proposed extending the estate by planting the lower meadows close to the river; but was told they were too saturated. She replied that they should import bog-draining fen-men from East Anglia – indeed, she knew just which trenchers to appoint; but was told that even were the slopes to be drained, the subsoil was inhospitable to vines.

Next she proposed the use of English horses to work the vineyard in place of oxen. M. Lambert took her into the estate and they waited at the end of a row of petit verdot as a pair of harnessed oxen, their heads cowled like nuns against the flies, progressed towards them. 'Look,' he said, his eyes shining, 'look how they pick up and put down their feet. Is it not as graceful as any minuet that has been danced in the ballrooms of Europe?' Emily responded with praise of the strength, docility and intelligence of English horses; and in this matter she had the bump of perseverance. A few months later a pair of sturdy, feather-footed shires arrived at Haut Railly. They were stabled, rested and praised. What went wrong thereafter she never quite discovered: were the horses too clumsy-footed, or the workers too little skilled at directing them? Whichever the case, the shires were soon living out a peaceful early retirement on the unplanted lower meadows of the estate, the frequent aim of pointed fingers from the Pauillac steamer.

This ferry, when not over-burdened, could sometimes be persuaded to put in at the château's bright new stone pier. Such piers, Emily discovered, were locally called *ports*. They were so named, she naturally deduced, because their intended function was not as a tying-up place for pleasure-craft, but as an embarkation point for goods: specifically and obviously, the estate's wine must in the past have been sent to Bordeaux for bottling by the direct water-route rather than being hauled overland. She therefore instructed M. Lambert to move the next vintage by this method, and he seemingly accepted the order. But a week later Florence informed her that the housekeeper had offered her resignation amid spectacular tears, because if Madame did not wish to employ her brother the haulier then she herself was unable to work for Madame, since her brother was a widower with many children, and reliant for their bread upon the haulage contract from the château. Florence had of course replied that they had known none of this, and Mme Merle was not to fret.

'Can the lazy fellow not turn to river haulage as well?' Emily asked rather snappishly.

'My dear, we did not come here to disturb their lives. We came for the tranquillity of our own.'

Florence had adapted to the Médoc with a swift content that was close to indolence. For her the year now ran not from January to December, but from one harvest to the next. In November they cleared the vineyard and manured; in December they lightly ploughed as protection against winter frosts; on January 22nd, St Vincent's Day, they started to prune; in February and March they ploughed to open up the vines; and in April they planted. June saw the flowering; July the spraying and trimming; August contained the *véraison*, that annually miraculous passage of the grapes from green to purple; September and October brought the *vendange*. As Florence watched these events from the terrace, she was aware of constant disquiet over rain and hail, frost and drought; but country folk were universally possessed by weather, and she decided as proprietor to exempt herself from such anxieties. She preferred to concentrate on what she loved: the vines draping their octopus arms over the supporting wires; the slow creak and tinkle as the sandy oxen made their stately way through the vineyard; the winter smell of a fire constructed from prunings. On late-autumn mornings when the sun rose low, she would sit in her cane chair with a bowl of chocolate, and from her flattened angle of vision all the rusting colours intensified: flame, ochre, and pale burgundy. This is our hermitage, she thought.

Each year for her therefore ended on the moveable feast

of the *bal des vendangeurs*. Mindful of M. Lambert's earlier strictures, Florence had in the summer of 1891 made several mysterious trips into Bordeaux. Their purpose became plain when she celebrated the second vintage of Château Haut Railly in resplendent evening dress: black barathea jacket and trousers, with white silk waistcoat underneath, all cut with an elegant eccentricity by a bemused French tailor. Emily wore the same yellow dress as the first year, and when the trestle-table feast was over, and the fiddles and squeezebox started up, *les dames anglaises* rose and danced to unfamiliar tunes of furious friskiness. Mme Florence threw Mme Emily around in passable imitation of the wiry, mustachioed *vendangeurs*, who for their part asserted the democracy of the dance-floor by defending their territory with shoulder and hip. At the end of an hour the two women found, in mid-dance, that everyone else had faded to the edge of their awareness, and they were the proprietors of empty space. When the music stopped, the other dancers applauded, M. Lambert drily clapped his hands, the youngest *vendangeuse* brought two bunches of heliotropes, Emily made her speech, which was not substantially different, except for an improved accent, from the previous year, and *les dames anglaises* retired to bed. Florence hung up her evening suit, which would not be taken down until the following year. In the dark, she yawned heavily and summoned up a final picture of Emily, half-blinded without her spectacles, being tossed and whirled about the courtyard in her yellow dress. 'Goodnight, *ma petite sulfureuse*,' she said with a sleepy chuckle.

The great crisis in the management of Château Haut Railly came in the summer of 1895. One morning Emily noticed the housekeeper's brother unloading barrels at the door of the *chai*. She watched the haulier without at first realising there was something inapposite about the way he heaved them from his cart and thudded them down on to the courtyard. Of course, it was obvious – it should have been immediately obvious – that the barrels were full.

When the haulier had departed she went to see the *régisseur*. 'Monsieur Collet, I have always understood that we make wine here.' The *régisseur*, a lanky, taciturn man, had fond respect for his employers, but knew that they preferred to approach any subject by an ironical or indirect route. He therefore smiled and waited for Mme Emily to arrive at the matter in hand.

'Come with me.' She led the way out into the courtyard and stood before the evidence. A dozen small barrels, neatly stacked, bearing no obvious stamp of identification. 'Where are they from?'

'The Rhone Valley. They should be, anyway.' When Mme Emily failed to respond, he went on helpfully, 'Of course, in the old days it was more difficult. My father had to bring Cahors down the Dordogne. Then they opened the railway from Sète to Bordeaux. That was a great advance.'

'Monsieur Collet. Forgive me, my question is this: if we make wine here, why are we importing it?'

'Ah, I see. *Pour le vinage.*'

Emily had not come across the term before. '*Vinage?*'

'To be added to our wine. To make it better.'

'Is this . . . is it . . . legal?'

M. Collet shrugged. 'In Paris people make laws. In the Médoc people make wine.'

'Monsieur Collet, let me get this clear. You, who are in charge of making our wine, you adulterate Château Haut Railly with filth from the Rhône Valley? You do this without permission? You do this every year?'

The *régisseur* could see that more than factual explanation was being called for. It was always the younger Madame who caused the problems. She had, in his opinion, a capacity for hysteria. Whereas Mme Florence was much more calm. 'Tradition is permission,' he replied. From Mme Emily's face he could see that the hallowed words of his father were not working their trick. 'No, Madame, not every year. Last year was a very poor vintage, as you know, so it is necessary. Otherwise no one will buy the wine. If it was a little better, we might be able to improve it with some of our own wine, a few barrels of the '93. That we call *le coupage*,' he added apprehensively, unsure whether he was compounding or diminishing his supposed sin. 'But last year was truly mediocre, so we need these helpful barrels . . . *pour le vinage*.'

He was unprepared for Mme Emily's next action. She ran to the store-house, returning with a mallet and chisel. A few moments later, a dozen holes had been made, and the lower part of Emily's dress was stained with a pungent, spicy red liquor of considerably greater vivacity than the 1894 Château Haut Railly stored a few dozen metres away.

M. Lambert, attracted by the mallet blows, ran from his office and attempted to calm Mme Emily by introducing an historical perspective to the situation. He told her about *les vins d'aide*, as they were called, and the preparation of wine for *le goût anglais*, as it was known in the Médoc, and how the wine that the English gentleman served at his dinner table was very rarely the same liquid that had left a particular estate a few months or years previously. He spoke of a Spanish brew called Benicarlo.

Emily's disbelief was like heat. 'Monsieur Lambert, I do not understand you. In the past you have lectured me severely about the purity of the Médoc vineyards, about how French vines must not be adulterated with American rootstocks. Yet you blithely throw barrels of . . . of *this* into what those self-same vines produce.'

'Madame Emily, let me put it like this.' His manner became avuncular, almost clerical. 'What is the best wine of the Médoc?'

'Château Latour.'

'Of course. And do you know the verb *hermitager*?'

'No.' Her vocabulary was certainly being broadened today.

'It means to put the wine of Hermitage, a wine of the Rhône as you perhaps know, into a red Bordeaux. To give it weight. To accentuate its virtues.'

'They do this at Latour?'

'Perhaps it does not happen at the château itself. On the Chartrons, in London . . . The négociant, the shipper, the bottler . . .' M. Lambert's hands sketched a conspiracy of necessary virtue. 'In poor years it has to be done. It has always been done. Everyone knows.'

'Do they do it there, next door, at Latour?' Emily pointed south, into the sun. 'Do the owners do it? Do they have barrels delivered like this, in broad daylight?'

The *homme d'affaires* shrugged. 'Perhaps not.'

'Then we shall not do this here either. I forbid it. We forbid it.'

On the terrace that evening, while her dress was still in the soak, Emily remained adamant. Florence at first tried to tease her into a good humour, expressing surprise that an enthusiast for transcendence should not wish her wines to enjoy this quality as well. But Emily was not to be humoured or flattered.

'Florence, you cannot say that you approve of this process. If the label of our wine proclaims it to be of a certain vintage, and it is in fact a mixture of two vintages, you cannot say that you approve?'

'No.'

'And you must therefore approve even less when our bottles contain wine from hundreds of kilometres away, grown God knows where and by God knows whom?'

'Yes. But . . .'

'*But?*'

'Even I, my dear Emily, have grasped that it is permitted to add sugar to our wine, and what is the name of that acid . . . ?'

'Citric acid, yes, and tartaric acid, and tannins. I am not sentimental enough to imagine that the process is not in some ways one of manufacturing. It is an industrial as well as an agricultural process nowadays. What I cannot abide, Florence, is fraud. Fraud on those who buy our wine, who drink it.'

'Surely people buy a wine because they know what taste it has. Or should have.' Emily did not reply, and Florence pursued her thought. 'An Englishman buys Château Latour with a certain expectation, does he not? So those who provide the taste he requires are merely giving him what he wants.'

'Florence, I did not expect to hear you taking the devil's position. I am perfectly serious about this matter. It seems to me of the utmost, the final importance.'

'So I can see.'

'Florence, we do not talk about such things, and I am happy that it should remain that way, but when we moved here, when we gave up the turnip-farmers, we did so, as I understand it, because we could not live pretendingly, shut up in all that cold formality, waiting for those four weeks of the year in which we might escape. We could not bear the fraud in our lives.' Emily by now had a lively blush and a stern stillness to her posture. Florence had seen her like this before, when she had the bump of perseverance about a matter.

'Yes, my dear.'

'You like to say that this is our hermitage. Well, so it is, but only if it is we who make the rules.'

'Yes.'

'Then we must not live pretendingly, or with fraud, or believe, as Monsieur Collet expressed it to me this morning, that "tradition is permission". We must not live like that. We must believe in truth. We must not live pretendingly.'

'You are perfectly right, my dear, and I love you for it.'

For once, M. Lambert and M. Collet were quite unable to prevail upon either of the Mesdames. Normally they knew to intervene with Mme Florence once Mme Emily was safely out of the way. They would address her with pathos or pride, invoke local or national considerations, and appeal to what they regarded as her essential complacency. But this time Mme Florence proved as obdurate as Mme Emily. Arguments from necessity and from tradition, references to the implied authority of the great vineyards, were placed before her in vain. There was to be no *vinage* and no *coupage*. There were to be no secretive deliveries of anonymous barrels, and, for that matter, no consequent obfuscations in M. Lambert's account books. Florence feared another threat of resignation, though far less than she feared the possibility of Emily's censure. But the two men, after several days of sulking and some growled conversations which seemed to contain more *patois* than usual, agreed that what had been ordered would be done.

The decade continued. The 1890s were kindlier years in the Médoc than the 1880s, and the last years of the century brought no sense of ending. Florence would reflect that their glass as yet contained no lees. They had settled comfortably into middle age, perhaps she more comfortably than Emily; and they had no regrets for England. Their stewardship of Château Haut Railly grew lighter. The replanting of the vineyard with ungrafted stock was complete; the oxen danced their minuets, the *vendangeurs* went through their ruffianly rituals. The old curé retired, but his successor respected the ancestral duties: tea in November, benediction of the vines in April. Florence took to tapestry work, Emily to pickling; they frequented the Bordeaux steamer more rarely. *Les dames anglaises* had ceased to be a novelty, or even an eccentricity; they had become a fixture.

Emily would sometimes reflect on how little impact they had truly made upon the estate; how little transcendence had occurred. They had brought money, to be sure, but this had merely allowed the vineyard to reassert itself, the better to take its chance against parasitical enemies and cryptogamic maladies. And at times like this, when she felt that personal will was less significant than philosophers claimed, she liked to think of human life as following its own viticultural cycle. Childhood was full of frosts and pruning, of wrist-cracking labour at the plough: it was hard to imagine that the weather would ever change. But it did, and June brought the flowering. Flowers led to fruit, and with August came the *véraison*, that miraculous colour-turn, the sign and promise of maturity. She and Florence had now reached the August of their lives. She shuddered to admit how much their maturity had depended upon the fortunes of the weather! She had known many who never recovered from the savagery of early frosts; others fell to mildew, rot, disease; others again to hail, rain, drought. They – she and Florence – had been lucky with their weather. That was all there was to say. And there the analogy ended, she thought. They may be now in their maturity, but there was no wine to be pressed from their lives. Emily believed in transcendence, but not in the soul. This was their patch of land, their patch of life. Then, at some point, the oxen came, dancing an unfamiliar dance, with the blade behind them cutting more deeply into the soil.

On the last evening of the century, as midnight approached, Florence and Emily sat alone on the terrace at Château Haut Railly. Even the familiar silhouette of the two elderly shires down in the lower meadows was missing. The horses had grown fat and nervous lately, and had been stabled close this night in case the fireworks alarmed them. *Les dames anglaises* had naturally been invited to attend the festivities in Pauillac, but had declined. There were times when the world shifted and you needed public comfort. But there were also great instants better savoured in private. Not for them tonight the official speeches, the municipal ball, the first purple-tongued riot of the new century.

Wrapped in rugs, they gazed down towards the Gironde, which was occasionally illumined by a premature rocket. A shuddery, but more reliable light came from the storm lantern set on the table between them. Emily could see that the balusters they had renewed a decade earlier had now quite blended in with the old ones: she could not now recognise, or remember, which was which.

Florence refilled their glasses with the 1898 vintage. It had been a small crop, reduced by lack of rain after a dry summer. The 1899, currently brooding in the *chai*, was known already to be magnificent, a grand finale to the century. But the 1898 had its virtues: a pretty robe, ample fruit, a proper length. Whether all these virtues were entirely its own was another matter. Florence, though essentially complacent, could not help being intrigued by the idea that their wine appeared to acquire a certain additional solidity between its journey in cask to Bordeaux and its return thence in bottle. Once, with a cheerful recklessness, she had ventured this notion to Emily, who had sharply replied that all good wine put on weight in the bottle. Florence had acquiesced in this declaration, and sworn to herself that she would never go near the subject again.

'You can be proud of this vintage,' she said.

'We can both be proud.'

'Then I give you a toast. To Château Haut Railly.'

'To Château Haut Railly.'

They drank, and walked to the front of the terrace, adjusting their rugs. They placed their glasses on the balustrade. The English grandfather-clock struck twelve, and the first fireworks of the new century climbed into the sky. Florence and Emily played at trying to guess their firing-points. Château Latour, obviously, that ruby explosion close at hand. Château Haut Brion, the browny-gold susurrus in the distance. Château Lafite, the elegant pattern to the north. Between the scatterings of light and the unfearsome crackles, they proposed a series of toasts. They turned towards England and drank; towards Paris; towards Bordeaux. Then they faced one another on the silent terrace with the storm lantern tickling their skirts and toasted the new century. A last, misguided rocket flew low across the water and exploded above their little *port*. Arm in arm, they walked towards the house, leaving their undrained glasses on the balustrade, and the lantern to burn itself out at some untenanted hour. Florence hummed a waltz, and they skittishly danced the last few yards to the French windows.

In the hallway, under the burner at the foot of the stairs, Florence said, 'Let me see your tongue.' Emily rather delicately extruded a centimetre and a half. 'Just as I thought,' said Florence. 'Stealing the grapes. Every year the same disobedience, *ma petite sulfureuse*.' Emily dropped her head in mock contrition. Florence tut-tutted, and turned down the light.

# TUNNEL

—————————————————— o ——————————————————

THE ELDERLY ENGLISHMAN was travelling to Paris on business. He settled himself methodically into his seat, adjusting the head-rest and leg-support; his back still ached from some light spring digging. He unfolded the table-flap, checked the ventilation nozzle and overhead light. He ignored the free magazine, audio-plugs and personal video facility with onscreen lunch menu and wine list. Not that he was against food and drink: he retained, in his late sixties, a hectic and at times guilty anticipation of the next meal. But he was allowing himself to become – or rather, to become to himself, rather than merely to others – a little old-fashioned. Perhaps it appeared an affectation to take home-made sandwiches and a half-bottle of Meursault in a cold-sleeve when lunch was provided free to business customers. But that was what he wanted, so that was what he did.

As the train eased grandly out of King's Cross he reflected, as he did every time, on the surprising banality that within his lifetime Paris had become closer than Glasgow, Brussels than Edinburgh. He could leave his house in north London and barely three hours later be heading down the mild decline of the boulevard de Magenta without even a flap of his passport. All he needed was his European identity card, and that only in case he robbed a bank or fell under the Métro. He took out his wallet and checked the oblong of plastic: name, address, date-of-birth, social security listings, phone, fax and e-mail data, blood-group, medical history, credit rating and next-of-kin. All these items, except for the first two, were invisible, encoded in a small iridescent lozenge. He read his name – two words plus an initial, all emptied of association after so many years of familiarity – and studied his photograph. Gaunt, long-faced, wattles under the chin, high colour and a few broken veins from disregarding the medical profession's advice on alcohol, plus the usual serial-killer's eyes that photo-booths inflict. He didn't think he was vain, but given his tendency to mildly disagree with most photographs of himself, admitted that he must be so.

He had first travelled to France fifty-six years previously, on a family motoring holiday to Normandy. No roll-on, roll-off ferries then, no Eurostar or Le Shuttle. They anchored your car to a wooden pallet on the Newhaven quayside and swung it into the depths of the ship as if it were a piece of merchandise. This habitual memory set off in him the catechism of departure. He had sailed from Dover, Folkestone, Newhaven, Southampton, Portsmouth. He had landed at Calais, Boulogne, Dieppe, Le Havre, Cherbourg, Saint-Malo. He had flown from Heathrow, Gatwick, Stansted, London City Airport; landed at Le Bourget, Orly, Roissy. Back in the Sixties he had taken an overnight sleeper from Victoria to the Gare du Nord. At about the same time, there had been the Silver Arrow: four and a quarter hours from city centre to city centre had been the boast, Waterloo to Lydd, Lydd to Le Touquet, and the Paris train waiting by the airstrip. What else? He had flown from Southampton (Eastleigh, to be precise) to Cherbourg by something called an air-bridge, his dumpy Morris Minor in the hold of a lumbering freight-plane. He had landed at Montpellier, Lyon, Marseille, Toulouse, Bordeaux, Nice, Perpignan, Nantes, Lille, Grenoble, Nancy, Strasbourg, Besançon. He had taken the autorail back from Narbonne, Avignon, Brive-la-Gaillarde, Fréjus and Perpignan. He had flown over that country, crossed it by train and bus, driven, hitch-hiked; he had raised broad-bean blisters walking through the Cévennes. He was the owner of several generations of yellow Michelin maps, whose slightest unfolding would stir him to vivid reverie. He still remembered his shock, forty or so years earlier, when the French had discovered the roundabout: bureaucracy meets libertarianism, that old French collision. Later they had discovered the speed-bump or sleeping policeman: the *ralentisseur* or *policier couchant*. Odd that our policemen slept and theirs merely lay down. What did that tell you?

The Eurostar broke from the last London tunnel into the April sunlight. Embankment walls of bistre brick noisy with graffiti slowly yielded to mute suburbia. It was one of those brittle-bright mornings intended to deceive: housewives pegging out their laundry were mistakenly in short sleeves, and young men would get earache from lowering their car-roofs prematurely. Xeroxed semis fled past his eye; prunus blossom hung as heavy as fruit. There was a blur of allotments, then a sportsground with a row of cricket sightscreens parked for the winter. He shifted his gaze from the window and picked at the *Times* crossword. A few years previously, he had announced his plan to ward off senility: do the crossword every day and call yourself an old fart if you catch yourself behaving like one. Though wasn't there something senile, or pre-senile, in these very precautions?

He turned away from himself and began to speculate about his immediate neighbours. To his right were three fellows in suits plus a chap in a striped blazer; opposite him an elderly woman. Elderly: that's to say, about the same age as himself. He said the word again, slid it around his mouth. He'd never much cared for it – there was something slimy and ingratiating about its use – and now that he was himself what the word denoted, he liked it even less. Young, middle-aged, elderly, old, dead: this was how life was conjugated. (No, life was a noun, so this was how life declined. Yes, that was better in any case, life *declined*. A third sense there too: life refused, life not fully grasped. 'I see now that I have always been afraid of life,' Flaubert had once conceded. Was this true of all writers? And was it, in any case, a necessary truth: in order to be a writer, you needed in some sense to decline life? Or: you were a writer to the extent that you declined life?) Where was he? *Elderly.* Yes, the fake gentility of that expression should go. Young, middle-aged, old, dead, that was how it went. He despised the way people pussy-footed about age – their own age – while happily thrusting it on others. Men in their mid-seventies referring to 'some old boy of eighty', women of sixty-five mentioning a 'poor old dear' of seventy. Better to err in the opposite direction. You were young up to thirty-five, middle-aged up to sixty, old thereafter. So, the woman opposite was not elderly but old, and he was old too: had been so for exactly nine years. Thanks to the medics, there was a lot of being old to look forward to. A lot of being as he now too often found himself: anecdotic, memorialist, rambly; still confident about the local connection between things but apprehensive about the overall structure. He was fond of quoting his wife's formulation, arrived at long ago when they had both been middle-aged: 'As we get older, we become hardened in our least acceptable characteristics.' That was true; though even knowing it, how could we be saved from it? Our least acceptable characteristics were those most apparent to others, not to ourselves. And what were his? One of them was complacently asking himself unanswerable questions.

He left the men till later. The woman: silverish hair which made no claim for authenticity (the colour, that is – the hair, as far as he could tell, was real), primrose silk shirt, navy jacket with primrose handkerchief in the pocket, plaid skirt which . . . no, he could no longer interpret hemlines in terms of fashionability, so didn't try. She was tallish, five eight or nine, and good-looking. (He refused that other slimy word, handsome. When applied to a woman above a certain age, it meant 'was once good-looking'. A harsh misapprehension, since beauty was something a woman grew into, usually in her thirties, and thereafter rarely grew out of. Brash, fuck-me innocence was something different. Beauty was a function of self-knowledge, plus knowledge of the world; therefore, logically, you would not be more than fragmentarily beautiful until you were thirty or so.) Why not a Crazy Horse girl? That would fit. She had the height, the bones, the grooming. Going back for a reunion: that's what they did, didn't they? Madame Olive's class of '65 or whatever. Odd that it was still going on, that despite the coarser sex-treats available there was still an audience for these hard-working English hoofers, matched like suburban semis, who danced what was held to be the tasteful erotic and weren't allowed to meet anyone within 200 yards of the club. He swiftly imagined her previous life for her: ballet school in Camberley, dancing on cruise-ships, an audition at the Crazy Horse; then came a spangly Latin stage-name, professional life in a family atmosphere, the club savings scheme; finally, after four or five years, back to England with the down-payment on a dress shop, gentleman admirers, marriage, children. He checked the wedding ring, which was centrally placed between two more geological items. Yes, that was about right, returning for the fiftieth anniversary . . . Madame Olive long since gone, of course, but Betty from Falmouth would be there, and so would . . .

The blazer of the fellow diagonally across from him was a bit bogus. Of course, all striped blazers were *au fond* bogus, pretending to be Jerome K. Jerome or Henley Regatta, but the ox-blood and lime elements in this one were approaching parody. A plump middle-aged chap with greying hair, side-burns and a noisy tan, yawning over a cycling magazine. Jack the Lad off for a spot of how's-your-father? Too clichéd. TV executive bidding for the coverage of this year's Tour de France? No, make a sideways jump. Antique dealer on the way to the Hôtel Drouot? Better. The jaunty jacket designed to supply a bit of false character, to help catch the auctioneer's eye yet also make rivals underestimate him when the bidding got serious.

Beyond the men in suits he saw an unstrung hop field and the half-cocked chimney of an oast-house. He pulled in his focus and tried to do the blokes justice. The one with glasses and a newspaper seemed to be examining the carriage window in some detail: all right, make him a civil engineer. The one without glasses but with a newspaper and a stripy institutional tie: third echelon of the European Commission? The other one . . . oh, count your prune stones: thinker, traitor, solderer, whaler . . . well, you couldn't do everyone, he'd already found that out.

In the old days – even in the elderly days – they might have been talking by this stage. The best you got nowadays was a sort of wary camaraderie. Stop. Old fart. That word *nowadays* is the giveaway, always preceding or following a statement worthy of denunciation by the absent, younger, critical self. As for the sentiment itself: you have been here before, don't forget. When you were a boy, adults were always boring on about how 'Everyone had *talked to one another during the war.*' And how had you reacted, becalmed in the throbbing boredom of adolescence? By muttering to yourself that war seemed a fairly high price to pay for this apparently desirable social result.

Yes, but even so . . . He remembered . . . no, that verb, he increasingly found, was often inexact. He seemed to remember, or he retrospectively imagined, or he reconstructed, from films and books with the aid of a nostalgia as runny as old Camembert, a time when travellers crossing Europe by train would become acquaintances for the length of the journey. There would be incidents, sub-plots, exotic characters: the Lebanese businessman eating currants out of a small silver box, the mystery vamp with a sudden secret – that kind of thing. British reserve would be overcome with the help of squintily suspicious passport inspections and the tinkly bell of the white-jacketed steward; or you might thumb open your tortoiseshell cigarette case and make social disembarkation that way. Nowadays . . . yes, nowadays the journey was too swift across this new European *zollverein*, food was brought to you at your seats, and no one smoked. The Death of the Compartment Train and Its Effect Upon the Social Interaction of Travel.

That was another sign of Old Fartery: thinking up wanly humorous thesis titles. Still . . . back in the early Nineties he had found himself in Zürich boarding an austere and unwelcoming train to Munich. The reason for its shabbiness soon became apparent: the final destination was Prague, and this was old Communist rolling-stock which had been graciously allowed to sully the impeccably capitalist track. In the window-seats were a tweeded Swiss couple, full of rugs, sandwiches and elderly suitcases (now that was all right, a suitcase could – even should – be elderly), which only a middle-aged Englishman was strong enough to heave into the rack. Opposite him sat a tall, blonde Swiss woman in scarlet jacket and black trousers, with a certain clunk of gold about her. Unreflectingly, he had gone back to his European edition of the *Guardian*. The train ambled bumpily over the first few kilometres, and each time it slowed the compartment door beside him would slide open with a bang. Then the train would pick up speed and the door hurtle itself shut with another uncushioned crack. One, two, or perhaps four silent curses were uttered every few minutes against some unknown Czech carriage designer. After a while the Swiss woman laid down her magazine, put on dark glasses and set her head back. The door banged a few more times, until the Englishman put his foot against it. He had to twist slightly to do so, and maintained this awkward, watchful posture for half an hour or so. His vigil had ended when a ticket collector rapped on the window with his metal punch (a sound he hadn't heard for decades). She stirred, passed up her ticket, and when the official had gone, looked across and said,

'Vous avez bloqué la porte, je crois.'

'Oui. Avec mon pied,' he had pedantically explained. And then, just as unnecessarily, 'Vous dormiez.'

'Grâce a vous.'

They were passing a lake. Which one was that? he had asked. She didn't know. Lake Constance, perhaps. She consulted the other couple in German. 'Der Bodensee,' she confirmed. 'It was here that the only Swiss submarine sank because they left the door open.'

'When was that?' he asked.

'It was a joke.'

'Ah . . .'

'Je vais manger. Vous m'accompagnerez?'

'Bien sûr.'

In the dining-car they were served by broad-hipped Czech nippies with tired faces and untreated hair. He had a Pils and a Prague omelette, she an unsightly mound of items topped off with a slice of beef, some bacon and a cruelly fried egg. His omelette seemed as delicious as this sudden situation. He had coffee, she a glass of hot water with a Winston Churchill tea-bag dangling in it. Another Pils, another tea, another coffee, a cigarette, as the soft south German countryside clattered past. They had disagreed about unhappiness. She said unhappiness came from the head, not from the heart, and was caused by the false images which arose in the head; he asserted, more pessimistically, more incurably, that unhappiness came solely from the heart. She called him *Monsieur*, and they addressed one another decorously as *vous*; he found the tension between this linguistic formality and the assumption of intimacy voluptuous. He had invited her to his lecture that night in Munich. She replied that she had been planning to return to Zürich. On the platform at Munich they had kissed on both cheeks, and he had said, 'A ce soir, peut-être, sinon à un autre train, une autre ville . . .' It had been a perfect flirtation, its perfection confirmed by the fact that she never came to his lecture.

The Shuttle terminal at Cheriton slipped by; the train manager announced that they were approaching the Channel. Fences, unsullied concrete, an inappreciable descent, then suave blackness. He closed his eyes, and in the tunnel of memory heard the echo of rhythmic shouting. It must have been fifteen, twenty years ago. Perhaps that dubious fellow across the aisle had set it off by summoning up his analogue. People repeated themselves, as stories did.

In the private darkness of his past, he turned and saw a group of football fans approach, beer can in hand, free fist aloft. 'Dra-gons! Dra-gons!' Black leather jackets, rings through their noses. Spotting grey-haired, comic-blazered Lenny Fulton, the smarmy yet opinionated presenter of 'Sportsworld UK'. Lenny Fulton, 'the man who likes to put himself about a bit', who earlier that season had denounced the less civil supporters of a south London club as 'worse than pigs' – 'indeed', he had gone on, 'to call them pigs would amount to a libel on that admirable beast.' Those accused had responded with satiric accord. You call us pigs? Very well, then pigs we shall be. In their hundreds they had turned up to the next match with brass rings clipped to their noses; the more ardent had their septums pierced and turned a fashion statement into a permanent declaration. From the terraces they had loudly oinked their support. Now they had found their condemner.

'Fucking Lenny! Look what we've got here!' There was a blur of movement, an inchoate roar, a spray of beer and a panicky squeak of 'Hey, lads', before Lenny Fulton was ripped from his seat and frog-marched away.

For ten minutes or so the other passengers looked around, mutually encouraging one another to do nothing. Then Fulton had reappeared with his guardians, who thrust him approximately back into his seat. He was dishevelled, red-faced, beer-haired and now wore a big brass clip-on ring through his nose.

'Fucking lucky, eh, Lenny? *Doors.*' One of the larger fans cuffed him across the face. 'Wear it, right, Lenny?'

'Right lads.'

'All the way to fucking Paris. *And* on TV. Be watching you.'

They turned to go, nose-rings glinting. On the back of their leather jackets were dragons' wings picked out in scarlet stitching. Lenny Fulton looked around his immediate companions and laughed self-consciously. 'Good lads, really. Just high spirits. It's a big match. No, good lads.' He paused, touched his nose-ring, laughed again, and added 'Fucking *animals*.' He ran his hands through his damp hair, back-combing it with his fingers until it stood up in a way familiar to viewers of 'Sportsworld UK'. 'If the doors weren't locked they'd have had me out. Pigs.' Then, with visible and melodramatic thoughtfulness, he appended the necessary qualification. '*Pigs* is too good for them. To call them pigs would amount to a libel on that admirable beast.'

They had urged calm and normality back upon themselves with talk of sport: the match against Paris Saint-Germain, the winter cricket tour, the Five Nations Tournament. He joined in awkwardly, asking one of his favourite questions: 'When was cricket last played at the Olympics, and who won the medals?' Lenny Fulton looked at him with the sort of professional suspicion he obviously reserved for sports bores. 'Trick one, by any chance?' No one hazarded an answer. '1900, Los Angeles, England the gold, France the silver. No bronze as those were the only two countries competing.' Only mild interest was expressed at this. Well, it had been more than a century ago. He didn't bother with his second question: what was the spot prize the year the Tour de France had passed through Colombey-les-deux-Eglises? Give up? All three volumes of General de Gaulle's memoirs.

When lunch arrived, the steward looked enquiringly at

Lenny Fulton and murmured, 'Up the Dragons, eh, Mr Fulton?'

'Fuck the Dragons, actually, from here to Timbuctoo. And would you refresh this with a quadruple. Single malt, none of your blended rubbish.'

'Yes, Mr Fulton.'

Now, years later, the elderly Englishman unwrapped his sandwiches, took out his travelling corkscrew and opened the half-bottle of 2009 Meursault. He offered a glass to the Crazy Horse girl opposite. She hesitated, took the bottle, turned it to read the label, and then assented. 'But just enough to taste.'

No one drank any more, he reflected. Or at least, no one seemed to drink as he did, just a little more than was recommended. That was the best way to drink. It was either quadruple whiskies and a softened brain, or else mimsy little 'tastes' such as the one he was now pouring. He imagined her back in her spangly days curling a little finger as she hoisted the *coupe de champagne* ordered by some hot-tongued admirer she had met 201 yards from the club.

But he was wrong. She wasn't going to Paris and she had never danced except on amateur nights. She told him she was going to Rheims for a vertical tasting of Krug back to 1928. She was a Master of Wine, and after holding his Meursault against the white tablecloth and briefly rinsing her mouth she declared that for an off-vintage it had reasonable fruit, but you could taste the rain and the oaking was rather out of balance. He asked her to guess its price, and her estimate was lower than what he had paid for it.

Well, a good misapprehension; not outstanding, but useful. His favourite was still Casablanca. Changing planes there on the way to Agadir some twenty years ago; scurrying through a sultry terminal, watching the boarding-lights begin to flash amid a loungeful of staid and stoic British travellers. Suddenly, a young woman had gone berserk and started upending her handbag all over the floor. Make-up stuff, tissues, keys, money fell out at their different speeds, and with a sort of manic defiance she continued hitting her bag long after it was empty. Then, very slowly, as if daring the plane to leave without her, she had started picking things up and putting them back. Her boyfriend remained stiffly in the queue while, furious yet unashamed, she rootled like a rag-picker.

They must have caught the plane, because they turned up at the same hotel, an oasitic place with snowy Atlas mountains rising behind sunlit tangerine groves. Walking to the bougain-villaea-draped main building on the first morning, he had noticed the girl sitting at a table with water-colour equipment strewn in front of her. His curiosity about what she might have lost at Casablanca airport was forcefully reactivated. Special factor-X sun-cream? Her list of local contacts? More than that, surely: something which had made her livid and her companion hot-cheeked. A contraceptive item whose absence would imperil the holiday? Insulin capsules? Colonic depth-charges? Henna rinse? He became retrospectively troubled on her behalf and quietly obsessed with the whole incident. He began inventing her life for her, filling the psychological dis-tance between raging traveller and calm water-colourist. For several days his speculations became more baroque as he pro-tracted his ignorance like a temptation. At last, his fear of losing what the girl knew – and what she doubtless failed to value at its true worth – became too much. He approached her one afternoon, banally praised her work, and then, with an awful, tense casualness, as if some chance of happiness were being wagered, asked what she had lost at Casablanca. 'Oh,' she had replied in a sharp, dismissive voice, 'my boarding card.'

He had wanted to bark with pleasure, but merely stood there like some desperate, pop-eyed fiancé, uncertain which delighted him the more: the excess of his misprisions or the primness of the truth. The following day she and her companion departed, as if they had fulfilled their function – which for him at least they had.

He looked out at the French landscape, idly attending to its sparse novelties. Thin drainage ditches and sleepy canals. Hilltop water-towers, some shaped like egg-cups, others like golf tees. Pencil-sharpened church spires instead of square English towers. A First World War cemetery waving a high *tricolor.* But his mind kept pulling back. Agadir: yes, that other misprision, half a century ago, when he had taught as an *assistant* in Rennes. That year of his life was now compressed in his brain to a few anecdotes whose final narrative form had long since been arrived at. But there was something else, not really an anecdote, and therefore likely to be a truer memory. His pupils had been friendly – or at any rate had treated him with humorous curiosity – except for one particular boy. He couldn't summon a name, a face, an expression; all that remained was the boy's place – back row, slightly right of centre – in the small, oblong classroom. At some point, and how it came about he no longer knew, the pupil had remarked point-blank that he hated the English. Asked why, he said because they had killed his uncle. Asked when, he said in 1940. Asked how, he said that the Royal Navy had treacherously attacked the French fleet at Mers-el-Kebir. You killed my uncle: you. To the young *assistant d'anglais*, the hatred and its cause had come as a complicating historical shock.

Mers-el-Kebir. Just a minute, that wasn't anywhere near Agadir. Mers-el-Kebir was near Oran: Algeria, not Morocco. Old fool. Old fart. You made the local connection but you missed the overall structure. Except here he hadn't even made the local connection. Hardened in your least acceptable characteristics. He rambled, even to himself. His train of thought had jumped the points, and he hadn't even noticed.

Someone handed him a hot towel; his face drained it to a cold damp rag. Start again. 1940: start there. Very well. 1940, he could safely say, was seventy-five years ago. His generation had been the last to have a memory of the great European wars, to have that sort of history entwined into its family. Exactly a hundred years ago his grandfather had set off for the First World War. Exactly seventy-five years ago his father had set off for the Second World War. Exactly fifty years ago, in 1965, he had begun to wonder if, for him, it would be third time lucky. And so it had proved: throughout his lifetime, his great, historical, European luck had held.

A hundred years ago, his grandfather had volunteered and been shipped out to France with his regiment. A year or two later he had come back, invalided out with trench foot. Absolutely nothing of his time there had survived. There were no letters from him, no buff field-postcards, no bar of silky ribbons snipped from his tunic; not a button, not a souvenir piece of Arras lace had been passed down. Grandma had developed into a zealous thrower-out in her later years. And this lack of the slightest souvenir was complicated by another layer of mistiness, of concealment. He knew, or thought he knew, or at least had believed for half his life, that his grandfather would talk freely about his enlistment, training, departure for France, and arrival there; but beyond this point he would not, or could not, go. His stories always stopped at the front line, leaving others to imagine frantic charges across the cloying mud towards a merciless greeting. Such taciturnity had seemed more than understandable: correct, perhaps even glamorous. How could you put the carnage of that time into mere words? His grandfather's silence, whether imposed by trauma or by heroic character, had been appropriate.

But one day, after both his grandparents were dead, he had asked his mother about her father's terrible war, and she had sapped his convictions, his story. No, she had said, she didn't know where in France he had served. No, she didn't think he had been anywhere near the front line. No, he'd never used the phrase 'over the top'. No, he hadn't been traumatised by his experiences. So why, then, did he never talk about the war? His mother's answer had come after a lengthy pause for judgment. 'He didn't talk about it because I don't think he thought it was interesting.'

And there it was. Nothing to be done about it now. His grandfather had joined the Missing of the Somme. He had come back, it was true; it was just that he had lost everything later. His name might as well be chiselled on the great arch at Thiepval. No doubt there was some regimental listing of him in a *livre d'or*, documentation of that absent strip of medals. But this would not help. No act of will could recreate that putteed and perhaps mustachioed figure of 1915. He was gone beyond memory, and no plump little French cake dipped in tea would release those distant truths. They could only be sought by a different technique, the one in which this man's grandson still specialised. He, after all, was meant to thrive on knowing and not knowing, on the fruitful misprision, the partial discovery and the resonant fragment. That was the *point de départ* of his trade.

Tommies they had been called a hundred years ago, while France was being deforested for trench props. Later, when he had taught in Rennes, he and his compatriots were known as *les Rosbifs*: an affectionate tag for those sturdy, reliable if unimaginative islanders to the north. But later still a new name was discovered: *les Fuck-offs*. Britain had become the problem child of Europe, sending its half-hearted politicians to lie about their obligations, and sending its civilian guerrillas to swagger the streets, ignorant of the language and haughty about the beer. Fuck off! Fuck off! Fuck off! The Tommies and the Roastbeefs had become the Fuck-offs.

Why should he be surprised? He had never much believed in the melioration, let alone the perfectibility of the human race; its small advances seemed to come from random mutation as much as social or moral engineering. In the tunnel of memory, Lenny Fulton's nose-ring was given a passing tweak, to a murmur of 'Up the Dragons, eh, cunt?' Oh, forget it. Or rather, take a longer view: it hadn't always been jolly old Tommies and Roastbeefs, had it? For centuries before, back to Joan of Arc (as quoted in the OED) they'd been Goddems and Goddams and Goddons, blaspheming ravagers of the happy land to the south. From Goddem to Fuck-off: not very far. And in any case, old men grumbling about rowdy youth: what a tired leitmotif that was. Enough complaining.

Except, complaint wasn't quite right. Did he mean embarrassment, shame? A little, but not mainly. The Fuck-offs had been an offence against sentimentality, that is what he thought he meant. Judgments on other countries are seldom fair or precise: the gravitational pull is towards either scorn or sentimentality. The first no longer interested him. As for sentimentality, that was sometimes the charge against him for his view of the French. If accused, he would always plead guilty, claiming in mitigation that this is what other countries are for. It was unhealthy to be idealistic about your own country, since the least clarity of vision led swiftly to disenchantment. Other countries therefore existed to supply the idealism: they were a version of pastoral. This argument occasionally provoked a further charge of cynicism. He did not care; he did not much care what anyone thought of him nowadays. Instead, he chose to imagine some French counterpart to himself, travelling in the opposite direction and gazing out at an unstrung hop field: an old man in a Shetland pullover entranced by marmalade, whisky, bacon and eggs, Marks and Spencer, le fair-play, le phlegme, and le self-control; by Devonshire cream teas, shortbread biscuits, fog, bowler hats, cathedral choirs, Xeroxed houses, double-decker buses, Crazy Horse girls, black cabs and Cotswold villages. Old fart. French old fart. Yes, but why grudge him this necessary exotic? Perhaps the true offence of les Fuck-offs had been the offence against this imagined Frenchman's sentimentality.

He had scarcely noticed the journey: countryside projected behind glass, twenty minutes of tunnel, then more projected countryside. He could have got off at Lille and visited the last surviving French slag-heap: he'd always meant to do that. There had been hundreds of anthracitic mounds gleaming black in the rain when he'd first come to this part of France. As the industry was run down, the abandoned heaps grew picturesque: green, suspiciously symmetrical pyramids such as nature would never craft. Later, some technique was found for pulping or liquefying the slag – he couldn't remember the details – and for some time now there had only been a single heap left, one stripped of its vegetation and showing its authentic blackness again. This remnant had become part of the Somme heritage trail: stroke the pit pony, study the diorama in which a black-faced miner stands behind glass like neolithic man, slalom down the slag-heap. Except that visitors were expressly forbidden to climb the heap; nor was any piece of slag to be removed. Uniformed guards protected the mineral as if it had true rather than assumed value.

Was this history coming full circle? No, a full circle was never achieved: when history tried that trick, it missed its orbit like a spacecraft piloted by someone who'd had too many bottles of this Meursault. What history mainly did was eliminate, delete. No, that wasn't right either. He thought about digging his vegetable patch in north London: you toiled and you lifted, and each year's double-spitting brought something different to the surface; yet the actual size of the surface remained constant. So you only uncovered that Guinness shard, filter-tip, bottle-top and ribbed condom at the expense of digging in other stuff from previous years. And what were they planning to dig in now? Well, there was a proposal before the European Parliament to rationalise the First World War cemeteries. All terribly low-key and respectful, of course, and larded with promises of sensitive democratic consultation; but he was old enough to know how governments operated. So, at some point, perhaps after his death, but inescapably, they would delete the graveyards. It would come. A century of memory is surely enough, as one smug debater had put it. Just keep a single example, following the established precedent of the slag-heap, and plough up the rest. Who needed more?

They had passed Roissy. A yardful of indolent commuter trains told him they were nearing Paris. The old red belt of northern suburbs. More iridescent graffiti on raw concrete, as in London. Except that here some Minister of Culture had declared the taggers to be artists, working in a form worthy to be set alongside the self-expressions of hip-hop and skateboarding. Old fart. It would serve him right if it had been the same Minister who had awarded him the green stud he now wore in his buttonhole. He looked down at it: another little vanity, like being dissatisfied with his photograph. He inspected his suit, which fitted him approximately: fashion and body profile kept moving in opposite directions. His waistband cut into an expanding stomach, while his legs had shrunk and his trousers hung loosely. People no longer carried string-bags for their shopping, but he remembered the way such bags would bulge eccentrically with vegetables, fitting their shape to the contents. This was what he had become: an old man lumpy and misshapen with memories. Except for a fault in the metaphor: memories, unlike vegetables, had a quality of cancerous growth. Each year your string-bag bulged the more, grew ever heavier, and pulled you lop-sided.

What was he, finally, but a gatherer and sifter of memories: his memories, history's memories? Also, a grafter of memories, passing them on to other people. It was not an ignoble way of passing your life. He rambled to himself, and no doubt to others; he trundled, like an old iron-wheeled *alembic* creaking from village to village and distilling local tastes. But the best of him, the strength of him, was still able to practise his profession.

The train made a polite, gingerly entrance to the Gare du Nord. In the tunnel of memory, Lenny Fulton skimmed his nose-ring under the seat as if he had never worn it, and raced for the door. The rest of them, memories and presences, here and elsewhere, nodded awkward farewells. The train manager thanked them for travelling Eurostar and hoped to welcome them on board again soon. Bands of cleaners stood ready to occupy the train and remove from it the faint historical detritus left by this group of passengers, preparing it for another group who would nod awkward greetings and leave their own faint detritus. The train gave out a vast and muted mechanical sigh. Noise, life, a city resumed.

And the elderly Englishman, when he returned home, began to write the stories you have just read.